IRRESISTIBLE

"Please," she said, "leave now, Billy."

"In a minute," he said on impulse, following an instinct he scorned in himself even as he obeyed it. "I haven't got everything I came for." He turned and sank onto the window seat, and tumbled her onto his lap.

Startled, Arlene lay still in his arms, hard, muscular arms that held her in an inescapable prison, pinioning her against the heat of his body. Then she reacted, trying to break free. "Billy, dammit, you have no right to touch me!"

"I know," he said, half-angry, half-rueful, "but when did I ever let that stop me?" He tangled a hand in her hair and tilted her head back, looking into her eyes for a long moment before he bent and claimed her lips. . . .

His mouth moved over her, harder than she remembered, far more expert, far more difficult to resist. Something in her cried out that if she did this, there might be no turning back, but then rational thought fled. . . .

BAD BILLY CULVER

Judy Gill

BANTAM BOOKS

NEW YORK · TORONTO · LONDON · SYDNEY · AUCKLAND

All of the characters in this book are fictitious,
and any resemblance to actual persons, living or
dead, is purely coincidental.

This edition contains the complete text
of the original hardcover edition.
NOT ONE WORD HAS BEEN OMITTED.

BAD BILLY CULVER

PRINTING HISTORY
Doubleday edition published March 1991
A Bantam Fanfare Book / September 1991

ISBN 0-553-29262-5

Published simultaneously in the United States and Canada

PRINTED IN THE UNITED STATES OF AMERICA

RAD   0 9 8 7 6 5 4 3 2 1

For Bob—
husband, lover, best friend,
and somewhat reformed juvenile delinquent

BAD BILLY CULVER

ONE

Billy Culver. Bad Billy Culver. He was back, twice as handsome and three times as charming, driving an expensive foreign import which, someone in Tulane's said, he'd probably rented for the day, just to show off. Somebody else hooted that idea down. Didn't they read the papers? Billy Culver was filthy rich, and as far as anybody knew, had gotten that way legally.

Billy didn't go into Tulane's, which was surprising. He'd been thrown out of the bar on more than one occasion. But he never tired of trying to convince the bartender that he was over twenty-one—when everybody in Oakmount Village knew he was nothing of the sort. It was a game to him. But then, most things were a game to Billy Culver. Maybe that explained why, now that he was definitely of age and then some, Billy didn't go into Tulane's: There wouldn't have been any sport in it.

What he did do was go to the Oakmount Village Public Library, where he leaned negligently on the counter, bent over and said softly, "Myrtle . . . oh, Myrtle, darling . . ." His singsong voice brought Miss Quail spinning around in her swivel chair, indignation brightening her normally paste-pale cheeks.

She gaped at him for a moment, then stood

quickly, not smiling. Not quite. "Billy Culver! To you, it's Miss Quail. And what might I ask are you doing here?" The crisp tone was completely at odds with the momentary softening of her eyes.

He handed her a book he'd had tucked under his arm. "Returning this. It's a bit overdue."

Miss Quail took it, opened it and blinked. "Yes," she said. "Seventeen years overdue." She squinted at the date again, her mouth tightening. "Thank you, Billy." Her tone was dry. "I'm happy to have it back." She turned away, marching, stiff-spined, back to her desk behind the counter, dismissing him.

"What about the fine?" There was laughter in Billy's voice.

She glared at him. "The book was written off many years ago. I'll simply treat it as a new acquisition. A donation." Once more she dismissed him by turning away and taking a huge ledger from a shelf over her desk and opening it across her blotter.

"I can afford the fine," he said, but Miss Quail merely addressed herself to the task at hand and wrote up the "new" acquisition.

What in the world had Billy Culver been doing with a volume of W. B. Yeats' poetry when he was only twenty? She considered asking him. She knew he hadn't left, knew, without having to look, that he was still leaning on the counter, grinning that cheeky grin of his, that his black curls were tumbled over his broad, intelligent brow. And she knew that she would find herself softening toward him again if she turned.

She turned. "What are you doing here?" she asked again.

"Visiting my favorite lady," he said, leaving the counter and sauntering in behind it to sit on the edge of her desk. Perched there, Billy looked into her eyes with the directness she'd always liked in him, and smiled that old knock 'em dead smile that had gotten him out of trouble all his life. "It's good to see you still here, Miss Quail," he said, and she heard the ring of sincerity in his deep voice. "I was kind of hoping you'd welcome me back."

With a sigh she patted his hand where it lay on his hitched-up knee. "All right, Billy. It's good to see you, too, but I'm one of the few who will say that. You don't have much of a reputation in this town. You're not staying long, are you?" She thought of poor little Arlene Lambert and hoped that Billy would do whatever he'd come to do—surely it was more than just returning an overdue library book—and go away again.

"A week, maybe. It depends," said Billy noncommittally. "I just got here. Are you trying to get rid of me so soon?"

Miss Quail didn't respond to that. She glanced out the window and gave his cream BMW an austere look. "I suppose that fancy toy is yours?"

"Like it?" He grinned with the same kind of pride he'd shown when Jenny, his mother, had given him that ugly secondhand bike for Christmas the year he was eight.

"Did you earn it honestly, Billy?"

His grin faded as he met her gaze. He nodded. "Yes, ma'am, and I worked hard."

For the first time since he'd come in, Miss Quail smiled at him. "Then I like it, Billy. I like it fine. Your mother would be proud of you."

Behind them, the door buzzed and two women entered, glanced quickly at the darkly handsome man sitting on Miss Quail's desk, and came to a halt, staring openly. Slowly, Billy leaned forward and kissed the librarian on the cheek, then got to his feet. Fingers in his hip pockets, palms facing outward, he strolled out from behind the counter, nodded politely to the women, then went on out

the door and got into his BMW. It purred to life and
was gone, leaving Miss Quail twittering and pink-
cheeked as she hadn't been since Admiral Forsythe
had kissed her at the civic luncheon last August,
when she received the award for Citizen of the Year.

As the two women wandered through the stacks,
Miss Quail sat at her desk, thinking back to when
she had been librarian in the island's private school,
Oakmount Academy, which Billy had attended from
kindergarten to the end of eighth grade. For the first
few years he was in school, Billy's quick intelligence
and sharp wit had delighted every teacher who dealt
with him. Sure, he was full of mischief, and often
went too far, but that was simply chalked up to his
being a little bit too smart for his own good. He had
to test the limits, not only of the rules, but the limits
imposed on him by his own body. He was athletic,
and too daring, and had to be the best at everything.
He was the first child in his group to "ride the
chute" on his bike. Some said he had discovered the
chute, perhaps even created it.

The trick entailed screaming along a narrow track
through the woods, flying blindly off the edge of a
short drop, landing exactly right on a plank at the
bottom of a wide ditch, then shooting straight up
the other side and onto the highway with no warning to oncoming motorists. Everyone was scared to
do it, but Billy had done it so the others had to
follow. It wasn't until Kevin Morrison II ran smack
into the side of the baker's van that the practice was
stopped. Billy, of course, was blamed for Kevin's
broken arm and concussion, just as he was blamed
four years later, when the boys were thirteen and
Curtis Hamilton dove headfirst off the swinging
bridge into the rocks of Skyline Creek Canyon
instead of into the deep pool he'd been aiming for.

If Billy Culver hadn't encouraged the other boys to dive there, Curtis would be alive today. At least, according to the gospel of Janine Hamilton, Curtis's bereaved mother.

Billy drove slowly through Oakmount, frowning at what he saw. Empty storefronts, newspapered windows, signs reading *Valuable Commercial Property for Sale*, or *Business Premises for Rent* or simply, grimly, *Closed*. On his way into town, he'd noticed how shabby everything had become, and how many For Sale signs dotted the residential streets. Of course, he'd heard all that from his advance team; he'd known Oakmount Village was ripe for the picking. But knowing it intellectually and seeing it firsthand were two different things.

He recognized faces, realized with shock that they belonged to people he knew, men and women who had been the boys and girls he'd gone to high school with. Only these people, many of them, looked, well . . . old. This was what Oakmount had become, then, a dying town populated by people without hope, with old gray faces, old gray lives. Before, the despondency he'd heard about, the imminent death of the town, had been nothing more than a piece of good news to him, a set of circumstances that would make the council more amenable to his plans. He knew the sawmill had gone from three shifts to two a couple of years back, and last year, to one, with the distinct possibility that within a few months it would close altogether.

But hell, he thought, shaking off the insipient sympathy he felt creeping up and putting on a burst of speed as he came parallel with the end of the bridge that led to Oakmount Island. That wasn't what he was there for. He didn't know exactly why he'd come, but it certainly wasn't to take a sentimental journey and start feeling any kind of pity for anybody in Oakmount—Village or Island.

Each community, in its own way, had shot Billy down as soon as it had a chance. First, the Islanders, because he was poor, because he was the son of a servant, because he didn't fit in exactly right. Then, after welcoming him, making him feel whole again, the Villagers had turned against him because he was supposedly too smart. He made them look and feel stupid, he'd been told. So to hell with them all. He flung back his head and laughed. "Let the bastards squirm."

Billy continued on around town, popping up here and there. He arm-wrestled with Stefan in the hardware store, and lost, of course, but with a grin that suggested he'd let it happen so as not to hurt the old ex-wrestler's feelings. He shot a few marbles in the dust with Carlie Malcolm's six-year-old twins outside her run-down dry cleaning business, then ducked into Mrs. Gaudin's dress store, of all places, and bought a bright pink silk scarf. Wherever he'd gone, he'd left folks laughing in his wake, or shaking their heads with questions in their eyes.

What was Billy Culver up to? Why had he come back?

And whom had he bought that pink scarf for?

He had dinner in the Markham Inn, the only "tablecloth" restaurant in town, served by Ellen Ames. She'd have served him more than dinner if he'd shown the least bit of interest, Billy thought. And he'd been pleased to see her, at first.

"Hey, Ellen! Hello. How's it going? It's a surprise, seeing you still here. I'd have thought there was a lot more of the world than Oakmount you'd want to see."

"I saw it," she said, her eyes growing predatory

as she gave him the once-over—twice. "But I didn't find anything like you out there, Billy Culver. If I had, maybe I'd have stayed away. But last time I got married, it was to Pete Mortimer. When his old man died, he decided to come back here and run the garage."

She smiled archly at Billy and cocked one hip, putting her belly too close to his face as he sat at the table. "Remember when you used to work there? Remember that black Ford van you test-drove after you repaired it? And you took me along? That was some test run, Billy Culver."

He nodded, wishing he could honestly say he didn't remember Ellen and the back of that van Amos Larson had rigged up for camping. "I didn't know old Mortimer had died," he said. "I'm sorry to hear it. How's Pete doing?"

"I wouldn't know. I'm not married to him anymore. He's not like you. He's content to run a garage for the rest of his life, and I can't stand a loser. I'll be gone again just as soon as I get a little money together. Or find somebody who wants to take me away from all this," she added breathily with another arch smile, thrusting her hips an inch or two closer to him. Her black skirt was tight and short and her white blouse cut low. Flesh spilled out of it. The dimples in her thighs showed even through her black fishnet stockings.

"I'm sure it won't take you long," he said.

"Damn right it won't. Then it's Vegas, here I come." She lifted her overtweezed brows toward the roots of her too-black hair. "You ever been to Vegas, Billy?"

He had, but shook his head, wishing she'd get down to the business of waitressing. He was hungry and not for what she was so blatantly offering.

"There's a good time to be had in that old town," she went on. "Tell you what, you say the word and

I'll get in that pretty car of yours with you and show you the sights of Vegas. And a few other things as well." She laughed so he could take her words as a joke if he chose, and she wouldn't lose face at his refusal.

He laughed too. "Why don't you show me the menu instead," he asked softly. "Then *I* can get out of *here*."

"You see that guy over there?" Ellen asked when she set his plate of pan fried red snapper in front of him. "The scrawny little bald guy having the drink in the corner by the fireplace?" He glanced over at the man she indicated. "You'll never guess who he's going to marry, Billy."

"Who?" he asked, looking up at her from his task of unwrapping the foil from his baked potato.

"Arlene. You remember Arlene Lambert, don't you?"

He swallowed dryly. Even if, by some miracle, he'd managed to forget Arlene, his wanderings through Oakmount that day would have provided a dozen reminders. Most people had mentioned her. Seemed she was a real heroine, beloved by all. He'd gotten sick of hearing what wonderful things she was doing, of how she had pulled herself up and become a real power in the community in spite of her reduced financial circumstances. He hadn't bothered to tell anyone that if Arlene had made good, she'd done so at his personal expense, by cheating him of what was rightfully his.

"Of course I do." His tone was bland, but his thoughts were sharp and spiky, hurting as thoughts of Arlene always did. Sly, cheating Arlene, who, as he should have expected, had grown up just like the rest of her family, greedy in spite of having everything handed to her. Or maybe because of it. Or maybe because of having lost it all when she did.

Whatever. She had cheated him, and he couldn't forgive that.

"Sam's my therapist, and we spend more time talking about Arlene than we do about me. She gave back his ring a couple of months ago, but he says she'll come around. She's just being coy. When I think about her and Sam together, I have to laugh. I mean, who'd have ever believed it?" Ellen said, openly gloating.

"Remember when she thought she was better than everybody? Like when she wouldn't even go to that dance with you when you'd told everybody that you were bringing her?" Ellen smiled a sly little smile.

Billy remembered that night, though it had been Arlene's grandpa, not Arlene, who'd refused him. He'd eased his hurt feelings in Ellen's eager softness. He wished now he could forget that, too. But how could he with her standing there so bold and open and clearly offering herself to him. Not that he took it personally. Ellen had always been man-crazy.

"Well, now she's like the rest of us—worse off, really. She's stuck with that shriveled-up old man, and teaching school for a living, and running a day care in her big, posh Island house. Poor Arlene," Ellen said, but her expression belied the words and tone. "Does she know you're back?"

"Not as far as I know."

"Do you plan to see her?"

"My plans are . . . flexible, Ellen. Look, I think that couple over there is trying to get your attention."

Flexible, hell, he thought, watching the provocative sway of Ellen's hips as she sauntered away. The one thing he did not intend to do during this short stay in Oakmount was drive over that damned class-dividing bridge to Oakmount Island and see Arlene

Lambert. Not for one solitary second. If she wanted to see him, she'd find out easily enough where he was staying. Hell, she probably knew now. A dozen people or more could be counted on to have rushed to the phone to tell Arlene that Billy Culver was back.

He put her way into the back of his mind and finished his dinner. Then, with nothing better to do, he went to the room he'd already booked in the Cozy Cabins Motor Court.

As he lay on his surprisingly comfortable motel bed, Billy thought again about his motives for coming back to Oakmount Village. He hadn't needed to be there. Everything was being done through intermediaries, and all was going as planned. He hadn't intended to come until the shouting and breast-beating was at its peak, so he could enjoy it to the utmost. How those Islanders were going to howl!

Billy laughed, linking his hands behind his head as he stared at the ceiling. If only they knew, those Islanders, Arlene first among them, that at any time he'd chosen within the last nine years, he could have come back and destroyed their peace of mind. But he hadn't done it. He'd waited, biding his time until he was fully capable of doing what he had long wanted to do. Now he was ready, and what he intended was something a lot more complex than destroying their peace of mind.

He was going to destroy their way of life.

He was finally rich enough, powerful enough, to do it. He liked being rich, for the most part, except that sometimes it was boring. No more good challenges. Another reason for coming back to Oakmount. To raise a little hell again, and to sit back quietly and watch it being raised, while nobody knew that he was the one to blame this time.

They'd always been so ready to lay the blame at his feet for anything, everything.

He scowled, wondering about Arlene, about how long she'd gone on hating him for what he'd done to her. That time, he *had* been the one at fault. He squelched the pang that always rose up when he thought about his last day on the Island, when he thought about Arlene, lying weeping in the grass. About him, walking away.

Too bad about her. She'd had her revenge.

Now it was his turn.

He grimaced and rolled over, reaching for his second cigarette in three years. The first had been an hour after dinner. This one was no better, he discovered as he lit it, drew deeply, coughed hard, and blew smoke out his nose. It stung. More of Arlene's revenge for what he'd done to her? If it was, it was unwitting, of course. She couldn't know that he'd quit smoking and now, just being within a mile of her had driven him to buy a pack of the damned things and start puffing away.

He snorted in disgust and took another deep drag that tasted and felt no better than the others. Never mind; now the revenge would be his. It was going to be very, very sweet.

Dammit, he couldn't keep his mind on that for some reason. Arlene kept intruding. Did she look as hard and as tired and as desperate as Ellen did? Or had she matured into the beauty her girlhood prettiness had promised? At thirty-four, she could be at the peak of her womanly perfection. She could be experienced enough to know what she wanted from a man, and how to get it. Did she get it from that damn geek she was engaged to?

The thought of Arlie coupled with that scrawny, bald-headed, middle-aged man suddenly made him sick. It made him mad enough to want to shake her silly, ask her what the hell she thought she was doing. Surely, she could do better than that? He hated thinking about it. He sucked in smoke again.

That thought had sent him out to buy the damn pack in the first place.

Oh, what the hell! What did he care? But waste bothered him. He ground out the half-smoked cigarette.

Sure. If waste bothers you so much, how come you're paying for a motel room when you have a place of your own to stay?

Because I can afford it, he answered, but that left him facing the question of whether or not he thought he could afford to go out to the Island.

"Of course I can," he said aloud, swinging his legs over the edge of the bed and getting to his feet. He shoved a hand into his pocket, where he carried The Key. He had carried it now for many years, like a talisman, and he always thought of it with capital letters. His lodestone, it had drawn him onward, upward, guided him when he might have faltered, and it had brought him back. It proved to him and to anyone else that he had a right to go to the Island.

"I can do anything I damn well please. Arlene Lambert is the guilty one. She's the one who should be scared. And that place is mine." He fingered the key to the gate that kept out the rabble, the key to a way of life available to the likes of Arlene Lambert. And now available to Billy Culver, by right of ownership, not simply because his mother performed a service or two for another landowner.

"I have as much right to cross that bridge as Arlene does," he told himself.

And if he didn't get up and cross it, he knew he'd go crazy lying there thinking about her, wondering, wondering, wondering. . . .

TWO

From her position on the window seat, Arlene saw Billy's car come up the drive, lights off. She knew who it was even though she'd never seen the car before. Enough people had called to let her know, the first being Miss Quail, speaking almost gently, Arlene thought, as if announcing a death, not a return. All she'd said was "Hello, dear. I thought you should know. Billy's in town."

Arlene had sat, staring at the phone, hearing the words but not quite understanding what the individual sounds meant. Something inside her had gone very still and quiet, watchful, as if waiting for the emotion she knew was about to sweep out of the darkness of her memories and overwhelm her with sensation.

With no expression she said, "Billy Culver?" and the first trickle began, tingling in her fingertips, forming a curl of heat low in her belly, a heaviness in the region of her heart, a humming in her head.

And a chilling, numbing fear.

Into the silence the dear old librarian had asked with concern, "Are you all right, dear?"

"Yes. Yes, of course, Miss Quail. Thank you for telling me." She smiled into the phone, keeping her face serene, knowing it would keep her voice calm, hiding even from herself the growing turmoil in her body, her mind, her heart. She must hide it! She didn't know quite why, but every instinct screamed at her not to react outwardly even though her mind was going into hysterics. *Billy? Billy back here? Did he know?*

Why hadn't she had some kind of psychic warning? An event of such momentous importance should have been presaged. How had she gone blithely through her day, working with the children, talking, discussing, laughing with the staff, without a presentiment of any sort?

"All right, then, if you're sure. Would you like me to come over? Or why don't you come and have a bite of dinner with me?"

"No, thank you, Miss Quail. I . . . I've eaten." It was a lie, but hunger was a long way from her mind. "I'll be fine. Please, don't worry about me." Even as she said it, though, she knew her old friend couldn't help but worry. Myrtle Quail knew, as much as anyone else in Oakmount, and more than most, what Billy was to her. And she to Billy. No, not was. Had been. *Had been!* But never, never again. And she was crazy, letting the news upset her like this. After all, seventeen years had passed. She'd had a crush on him when she was a kid. She'd thought she was in love with him. But a seventeen-year-old doesn't know the first thing about love. *And do you now, at thirty-four?* She brushed the question aside, refusing to hear it. She knew only that what she had once felt for Billy Culver was dead and gone—or it damned well better be! She'd hung up moments later, trying to assess exactly what it was she felt.

Finally she decided—about the same time Sam Burgoyne called to tell her about Billy. "I don't feel anything," she'd said in response to his question. Sam didn't know her half as well as he liked to think he did, or he'd have recognized the lie. She laughed hollowly at his suggestion that they reinstate their engagement for the duration of Billy's stay, so Sam could "protect" her and Marcy from the interloper.

"Thank you, Sam, but no. Believe me, I need no protection against Billy Culver."

"Well, if you're certain. But if you change your mind about the way you feel, let me know."

"As I told you, I feel nothing. Good night, Sam. Thank you for caring."

Nothing? Nothing? How could she have said that with such believable conviction? What she felt was a drumming sense of excitement along with fear and guilt and a longing for something utterly impossible. She felt that way whenever she let herself remember Billy, which was why she kept him tucked away in the back of her mind most of the time. Pulsing, drumming excitement that had no outlet made life uncomfortable, and the guilt became unbearable if she let herself focus on it.

Her years of treatment had given her the inner strength not to dwell on things over which she had no control, things for which she was not responsible. But it was a strength that could be sapped if she weren't careful. She would have to keep reminding herself that what she had felt for Billy Culver was far, far in the past, and these twinges were nothing more than fantasy. There was no other way to account for the intensity of the feelings sweeping through her—the deep and powerful throbbing that wouldn't stop, the hammering of her heart, the pounding in her blood of an endless chant that repeated over and over. *Billy, Billy, Billy . . .*

The moon shone on the cream paintwork and sleek chrome of the car in her driveway, and its shape gave away its make, its high price. She had a glimpse of dark curls, a chiseled profile, a broad shoulder as the car's dome light came on with the opening of the door and Billy got out. He headed for the porch and the front door. She sat there, wondering if she would respond to his knock.

When it came, she put her feet down and stood on surprisingly steady legs, and without thinking much about it, went into the foyer. She turned on the exterior lights and opened the door.

"Hello, Arlie." His face, shadowed as he bent his head to look down at her, was unreadable. His voice was deeply resonant, huskier than she remembered. He seemed taller, broader, maybe even a bit intimidating, but still a wash of the old familiar feelings warmed her insides and brought a smile to her lips. She firmed them into a straight line and straightened her back. She couldn't afford any kind of weakness where he was concerned.

"Billy." Her voice was cool and unsurprised, holding almost, but not quite, a question.

He'd expected her to be nervous or even angry, so the imperious tone, the upward intonation, startled him. She sounded, he thought with a short-lived burst of amusement, much like her grandmother had when he was a child. Gracious, polite-if-it-killed-her, but not particularly welcoming toward her housekeeper's son.

"May I come in?" he asked.

"No." She glanced down at the flowing white nightgown that covered her from neck to toe, from wrist to shoulder. "As you can see, I'm not dressed for company."

"I think we need to talk, Arlie."

"Arlene," she corrected him. "Nobody calls me Arlie anymore."

How could someone nearly a foot shorter than he look down her nose at him, he asked himself. Yet she managed it. It angered him, and somehow touched him at the same time.

"I do," he said, giving into the impulse to stroke her cheek with two fingers. Her skin felt warm, alive, pliant, and young, and his body tightened in response. He quickly dropped his hand. Dammit, he was reacting as he had long ago. It was memory doing that, nothing present-day. And it ticked him off. As much as the thought of that young, alive skin being touched by that dried-up old man he'd seen in the Markham Inn.

He saw that she, too, was angered by something. A sexual response to his touch, as automatic as his own had been? Her eyes flared briefly with hostility at his impudence, but she didn't flinch, only continued to meet his gaze until he was the one who looked away. Then, and only then, did she step back, not in invitation, he knew, but to put distance between them. She still had one hand on the door, the other on the frame, blocking his way.

"Arlie—Arlene, we do have things to discuss," he said tightly.

"But not tonight."

He saw her swallow, her slender throat working, her gray eyes wide and full on his face, capturing the light and reflecting it back at him. She was as beautiful as he'd anticipated, her face thinner, features more defined, her hair not so long, but hanging loose around her shoulders as he'd remembered.

"Yes, tonight," he said, his tone hardening, letting the anger come back to strengthen his resolve.

"What?" she asked imperiously. "What could we possibly have to discuss that can't wait for a civilized hour?"

He smiled, a slow and sexy smile that he'd practiced over the years with excellent results. Hell, he'd first learned of its efficacy by using it on her. His gaze locked with hers intimately. At first it had no apparent effect, then suddenly her mouth trembled for an instant and her eyes darkened involuntarily in response. She looked young and dewy and vulnerable, standing there in her nightie, and he hadn't anticipated the impact her vulnerability would have on him. It made him doubt himself, doubt the rightness of his plans to include her in whatever he did to the Islanders, and he couldn't afford that. She was one of them. She was the *worst* one of them. She had pretended the longest to be his friend.

She took another step back, and he experienced a moment's triumph, as brief as the flare of response he'd seen in her. Then her chin tilted, and she looked down her nose at him again, being Ms. Rich Bitch, which she most definitely was not! She was no longer entitled to her haughty manner, and he wasted no time in reminding her.

"You damned well know what we have to discuss," he said, the surge of anger in his breast adding harshness to his tone. He lifted her barricading arm and forced his way into the foyer. "Your theft of my property, Arlie, is what's on my mind. Don't you think you've gotten away with it long enough?"

His property? The cottage? That was all? Relief made her weak, and Arlene gripped the back of a chair to steady herself as Billy closed the door behind him. Still, she had to be sure. "What do you mean?"

He laughed softly, the sound wrapping itself around her. He stepped closer, and automatically, she moved back again.

"Invite me in, and I'll tell you what I mean. Assuming I really need to."

Invite him in? He was already in, and she still wasn't exactly sure how it had happened.

She turned and led the way into her sitting room, pausing beside the window seat when he hesitated in the doorway, looking around before entering. Standing before a sofa a few feet away from her, he gave her a quizzical look. "Didn't this used to be the dining room?"

She nodded, but gave no explanation. He shrugged out of his denim jacket without invitation and draped it over a straight-backed chair by a drop-leaf walnut table. He walked farther into the room, eyes blatantly curious to see what changes had been wrought since the Lamberts lost their money.

As he came into the brighter light, Arlene caught a silent breath. Before, as a boy, he had been handsome, well-built, tall. Now, a mature man, he was . . . magnificent. His shoulders were broad, the fabric of his shirt strained by the muscles of his upper arms and chest. His narrow waist tapered into even narrower hips, and long, powerful legs. Vitality gave his skin a healthy glow and a few white strands in his curly blue-black hair caught the light, sending shimmering shafts outward.

His rich blue eyes captured her gaze for a moment, slid over her face almost in a caress, down her shoulders, and over the voluminous folds of her gown, as though assessing what was under the yards of cloth. They rested for an instant on the pale pink polish of her toenails before rising once again to her face. She drew in a long breath and tried to let it out slowly, her eyes caught and held by something compelling in his deep blue gaze.

"Have a seat," she said finally. "I'll go get dressed."

"No," he said, catching her hand as she began to turn away. "There's no need." He took her other hand and held both her arms out from her sides. She was struck by the warmth of his hands, by their callused hardness, by the power she could feel in his fingers as they held her hands gently but firmly, not letting her escape. A pulsing thread of memory curled through her body, and she tugged to free her hands, but not hard. The memory remained, and his voice, soft, deep, and seductive, enhanced it.

"You've grown up to become a very beautiful woman, Arlie. Of course, that was inevitable, given your looks as a girl." He gave her a devilish grin. "Too bad you're wearing that tent. Did your body live up to its potential as well?"

"That's none of your business!" She snatched her hands free and whirled, the white gown swirling around her legs, pressing against her thighs, her bottom, her waist, as she unwittingly showed him exactly what her womanly shape had become. He whistled, a long, low tone of appreciation.

"Very nice," he said behind her.

She turned slowly and glared at him before moving to a side table. How could she go and get dressed? She didn't trust him not to follow, to burst in on her. He didn't look like a man who'd be stopped long by a locked door. She swallowed hard, remembering how he had climbed a maple tree to gain access to her room when they were children.

The tree was still there.

"Sit down," she said once more. "Will you have a drink?"

To his surprise and chagrin, the beginnings of an old craving filled his mouth with a never-forgotten taste. He swallowed hard, his throat dry. Once, he had been able to drive out one craving by submitting to another. Now he would give in to neither.

"No, thanks," he said, and sat in an armchair, shoving a footstool aside.

He recalled how her grandmother had always put her small, well-shod feet exactly together on a low stool before her, and sat with her back completely erect, even in an upholstered chair. She had been a little woman, and while Arlene was not over average height, she had been, by the age of eleven, as tall as her grandmother, then in her teens, taller.

Arlene sat now, as her grandmother had, but without the stool, her bare feet planted solidly in front of her, her back rigid, her chin high. "Well," she said. "You called me a thief. I suggest you explain."

"Do I need to, Arlie?" From his hip pocket he withdrew a folded sheaf of papers. "A copy of my mother's will, leaving me all her possessions. Also, a copy of the deed to the cottage, which your grandfather left to her . . . or, in the event of her prior death, to me. What I want from you is the key, and I think I'm the one owed an explanation. Your grandfather died sixteen years ago. You've known since then that the cottage was mine. Why did you never let me know?"

Again, relief rocketed through her. It was all right. It *was* only the cottage he wanted, not Marcy. A spasm of grief squeezed her as she thought that if Billy wanted to live here, she could not—not and keep Marcy safe from him. She'd spent her life protecting her daughter. She'd give it to continue doing so. She would also give up her home and the other children she cared for if that was what it took. Marcy came first.

She forced herself to breathe, found the strength to get to her feet and walked steadily to the rolltop desk at the far side of the room. She fished in a pigeonhole for a key and unlocked a lower drawer. After a moment's search she unearthed a key on a string with a tag tied on it and turned, dangling it before her.

She brought it to him, dropping it into his hand, and then continued to stand, pointedly. If he'd been a gentleman, he wouldn't have remained seated while she stood, but he was not. He never had been, though his mother had tried to make him one. Not being a gentleman made life a lot simpler, he had decided years before. It helped him get what he wanted.

"There's the matter of the explanation," Billy reminded her. "You may as well sit down again and get it over with, because I'm not leaving until I have it." He waited patiently until she complied, at least with the seating arrangements he wanted.

"Why did you and your family fail to inform me, or have me informed, that your grandfather left the cottage to my mother?"

"I . . . wasn't present at the reading of my grandfather's will."

He lifted his brows. "Are you telling me that your father and grandmother didn't tell you the cottage was mine?"

She said nothing, only looked at him with those level, steady, gray eyes masking her thoughts.

He sighed. "All right. I can see you aren't going to answer. When did you first know who owned the cottage?"

He thought for several moments that she was going to treat that question as she had the one before it. Then, in a quiet voice, she said, "After my grandmother's death, eleven years ago."

"I see. And didn't you think I had a right to know?"

"I didn't know where to find you. If you recall, you left here the day of your mother's funeral. You never wrote, never phoned, never got in touch with anyone in Oakmount again . . . until today."

He closed his eyes briefly, trying not to think of the loneliness of those first years, how difficult it had been to stay away. But he'd had to do it. It was the only way. "I wasn't in hiding, Arlene. And for the past seven or eight years I haven't exactly kept a low profile. If you'd wanted to find me, you could have."

"I didn't want to."

The hurt hammered through him. "Well, that's to the point, isn't it?"

"You'll find the cottage in good repair, and clean. It's still fully furnished, of course." She moistened her lips with the tip of her tongue, and his groin tightened. He ignored that pain, and it lessened in the greater pain her next words brought. "I packed all your mother's things for you," she said.

"Thank you."

For a moment they simply looked at each other, both involuntarily remembering the day of Jenny Culver's funeral, how he had wept in Arlene's arms, and said he didn't know what to do about his mother's things. At the time, neither of them knew that the cottage in reality belonged to Billy. They'd both believed he had to vacate it as her father had ordered. As much as Arlene had wanted him to stay, as hard as she'd begged, they'd both known it was impossible. He was persona non grata.

"Arlie . . ." His voice cracked and he cleared his throat. Before he could finish what he had started to say, she jumped up and drew the drapes around the curve of the bay window. When she turned to address him, her voice was higher than normal.

"They're still there," she said. "Her things. I didn't know what to do with them when I . . . after I packed them. And no one was using the cottage, so I just left them. They're all in boxes. I've kept the place heated, and seen to it that the taxes were paid each year since my grandmother's death."

He got to his feet and came closer. "It was kind of you to keep her things," he said. "Especially when you didn't know the place was mine. Why didn't you rent it out? It would have meant extra income for you."

"I've known for eleven years that it was yours, that it wasn't mine to rent out."

"But no one else did," he said softly, coming a couple of steps closer. "Or if they had, they wouldn't have cared what you did with it."

"Obviously, you knew." She raised her chin. "Why didn't you come to claim it long ago?"

He met the challenge in her calm gray eyes, wondering if they'd remain so calm once she learned the truth. He hadn't known for nearly two years after her grandmother's death that the cottage was his. "I wasn't ready."

"And now you are?"

He shrugged. "As ready as I'll ever be."

"Will you be moving in? Do you plan to stay here, Billy? On Oakmount Island?" He heard the nervousness in her tone.

Again, his big shoulders moved negligently. Until she'd asked the question, he hadn't really considered it. Now he said, "Maybe. For a while."

He was just toying with her, he told himself; he didn't really mean it. But when her face went pale, and a feverish color rose in her cheeks, he felt compelled to say, "Why? Don't you want me here?"

Of course she didn't. She probably didn't care one way or another about him now. Feelings such as they had shared did not last for nearly two decades, not unless they were bolstered and nurtured and reinforced. Anyway, she ignored that question. "What about your . . . businesses?" she asked tautly.

So she knew there was more than one. That showed she'd been paying some attention to the news about him. "I've retired," he said.

She raised her brows and tossed her head, her honey-colored hair tumbling against the shoulders of her white nightgown. She looked downright virginal. If he didn't know better, he'd have believed the illusion she projected.

"Retired? At thirty-seven?"

He laughed. "Why not? I'm rich enough."

She didn't dispute or question that. "Are you selling your business interests?"

"Probably not. But other people can look after them." He moved in on her and took her hand again. She tried to tug it free, but he encircled her wrist in his long fingers. "I have other things I want to take care of."

Her heart hammered high in her throat again, choking her. What things? Part of what she felt was fear, part . . . something else, something she didn't want to feel. She refused to acknowledge it. "I see. Fine then. I won't keep you chatting any longer, Billy. It was good of you to drop by, and I apologize for the delay in getting the key to your cottage to you. Good night."

He laughed, a little more loudly this time. "Just like that? Do you have any idea how much like your grandmother you've become, Arlene? In manner, not looks. You can't simply dismiss people that way, you know. What if I'm not ready to leave?"

"This is my home, and I decide who stays and for how long," she said with that same imperiousness that had intimidated him in her grandmother, and now, in her, simply amused him.

"Is that the way you treat your fiancé?"

"I have no fiancé."

"No? According to Ellen Ames, you do. She pointed him out to me. An old guy without much hair," he added, dismissing the man with his negligent smile.

"That's Sam Burgoyne, an old friend. I was engaged to him very briefly last year, but we agreed that it wouldn't work."

"Why wouldn't it have worked?"

She didn't answer that, merely said, "Billy, I'd like you to go now. I have a busy day tomorrow."

He nodded, but continued to hold her hand, continued to stand there looking down at her, his beautiful mouth curved into a smile that she sensed could turn hard at any moment.

"So tell me, why does Ellen think you're still engaged? More to the point, why does Ellen's therapist think you're going to marry him when you're all done being coy?"

"I'm not responsible for Ellen Ames' beliefs."

"But you are responsible for Sam Burgoyne's. Why haven't you managed to convince him that it's all over? Do you still sleep with him?"

"My private life is none of your business!" She felt her heartbeat in every inch of skin, but nowhere more than under the hand Billy had wrapped around her wrist. She heard its echo in her voice. Hoping he hadn't heard it too, she spoke more firmly. "Good night. You've got what you came for." She tugged against his hold but he refused to let go. "Please," she said. "Leave now, Billy."

"In a minute," he said on impulse, following an instinct he scorned in himself even as he obeyed it. "I haven't got everything I came for." He turned and sank onto the window seat, and tumbled her onto his lap.

Startled, Arlene lay still in his arms, hard, muscular arms that held her in an inescapable prison, pinioning her against the heat of his body. Then she reacted, trying to break free. "Billy, dammit, you have no right to touch me!"

"I know," he said, half-angry, half-rueful, "but when did I ever let that stop me?" He tangled a hand in her hair and tilted her head back, looking into her eyes for a long moment before he bent and claimed her lips.

She refused to open her mouth, but he managed somehow to find a way in, and she quivered in his hold as his lips took hers, firm and demanding and incredibly sweet. His kiss was sure, the kiss of a mature man who knew what he wanted and meant to have it, and she recognized at that moment she was lost.

His mouth moved over hers, harder than she remembered, far more expert, far more difficult to resist in its quest for her tongue. It felt like heaven, and she struggled not to give in to the pounding in her blood that demanded she succumb totally to the heady delight his touch brought her. There was something she had to think about, something she needed to remember, but all of that was fading away, dwindling to meaningless mush in her mind. She sighed silently and kissed him in return.

Something in her cried out that if she did this, there might be no turning back, but then rational thought fled and she molded herself to him, pressing her yearning body to his, searching for the elusive, unique sensation he had once unleashed in her. And it was there, growing, tormenting her with such a need that she cried out from the pain of it. Her fingers, gripping his shoulders, were icy cold while her body flamed from within.

Time had lost meaning when, slowly, Billy lifted his head, stroked a thumb over her swollen, wet lips, and ran a shaking hand into his curly hair. He looked as stunned as she felt, and murmured, "Oh, baby . . ." in a shaken voice.

Baby? Oh, God, what was she doing? How could she have forgotten, even for a moment? She tore herself free, pushing her way out of his arms, off his lap, putting half the room between them. "No!" she shouted when he began to follow her. "Don't touch me!" She turned away from him, arms wrapped around her middle, head bent, hair curtaining her face. "Go," she said. "Just get out of here, Billy."

"All right," he said, close behind her. "But I'll be back."

She felt a feather-light touch on her nape and shuddered—not in pleasure.

She turned, lifted her head, and stared at him defiantly. "Don't bother. There's nothing here for you."

"I'm not so sure about that," he said, giving her a long, hard look. "Maybe we have more unfinished business."

"We do not."

"Why? Because maybe the old goat thinks he has prior claim? I don't think either of us will let him stop us if we decide we want each other again. For my part, this little session came pretty close to changing my mind about you, and what I mean to do to you."

She stared at him, ignored his suggestion that her engagement was still on. "What are you saying?"

Oh, hell, what *was* he saying? She'd gotten him so damned rattled, he wasn't even thinking! If he didn't shut his mouth, he'd blow the whole deal long before he was ready to make it public.

"I'm saying I came back here looking to hate you, Arlie. Now I find I don't. Or not as much as I thought. Sure, you cheated me, but I remember a day when I cheated you too. Maybe I think I owe you something for that."

She frowned. "What day? You owe me nothing."

"I took something from you," he said slowly. "And I gave you nothing in return." He touched her cheek as he had after his arrival. "Your kisses tell me maybe you're still looking for it."

Her eyes widened as she began to understand. "Get out!" she said in a harsh whisper. "And don't come back! I want nothing from you, Billy Culver, nothing but your absence."

He shrugged. "Maybe I want something for you."

She misheard. "What do you want from me? Sex?

You can get sex anywhere, Billy, and I'm certain you do. Or are you pretending to look for love? Don't make me laugh. We were little more than children when I offered you my love. I didn't know what it was, or what I was saying. And what I felt then is long since gone."

"I said maybe I want something *for* you, Arlie, not from you."

"It's not your place to want things for me," she responded angrily. Striding to the front door, she swung it open in an unmistakable gesture of dismissal. "I've been providing for my own needs for a long time, and will continue to do so."

He joined her in the doorway, but still didn't leave. "Your needs aren't being met, not all of them, or you wouldn't have responded like that in my arms. I saw the old man you were engaged to. For God's sake, why don't you find somebody young, Arlie?"

She glared haughtily. "I suppose you're offering yourself?"

He laughed. "Not on your life, baby. I learned my lesson years ago. That kiss was a momentary madness. Oh, it was great, and I know we'd do fine in bed together. We might even get there, but only for laughs—not for life. That's the way I take my women now. But what kind of a life will you have with such a worn-out old man?"

"Dammit, I'm not going to marry Sam, not that my life is any of your business! Get out, Billy. Go!"

"Sure," he said. "But I won't be far away." He bounced the key to the cottage in his hand as he gave her another searching look. "I want all that belongs to me, Arlie. And I mean to have it."

He left her standing in the doorway. She closed the door against the January chill and watched from the window as his car turned and circled out of the driveway. He didn't head for the cottage as she'd expected, but for the bridge and the town over the inlet.

She stirred herself and went to bed, wishing she could sleep because she hadn't been making excuses when she told Billy she had a busy day ahead of her. She did need to rest, but she knew it wasn't to be.

What did he mean, all that belonged to him? How much more did he know? He'd kept his knowledge of his inheritance to himself until he was ready to take it. What else was he not telling her? What else was he holding back . . . until he was "ready"? She wrapped her arms around herself and considered what other disasters could befall her.

Billy Culver's return meant nothing good for her. Of that, she was very certain.

THREE

Stupid, stupid, stupid. Billy berated himself. He rolled off his bed and went into the bathroom, where he showered, cold, for the second time since he'd come back from the Island hours before. He couldn't sleep. He couldn't quit thinking. He couldn't quit remembering. What he needed right now was a quick dose of reality. Wrapping a towel around his hips, he went dripping back to the bedroom, sat down and picked up the phone, dialing swiftly and from memory.

"Dammit, Billy, it's two o'clock in the morning!" answered a sleepy voice.

"How'd you know it was me?"

"Who else calls me at two A.M.?"

"Who else do I pay to answer the phone at two A.M.?" Billy countered.

"Yeah, right. So, what's wrong? Do I need to bail you out of some local sheriff's hoosegow?"

"Nope. Leave your lawyer hat in the closet. All you need tonight is your guardian hat. I figured you should know where to reach me in case Holly needs me."

"You're no longer in Portland?" Glenn sounded alert now, and suspicious. He usually sounded suspicious when questioning Billy. He was worse than a jealous wife.

31

"That's right. I left there this—yesterday—morning. On impulse, you might say."

There was a pause, then Glenn asked, "So? Where can I reach you?"

The pause sounded cautious, Billy thought. But that was fine. He paid Glenn a lot of money to be cautious and thoughtful. And suspicious. Though not of him. "The Cozy Cabins Motor Court. Unit six. Oakmount Village, Washington," he replied, and waited for the explosion.

"Oakmount?" The explosion came right on schedule. "What the hell are you doing in Oakmount? I thought you were going to leave negotiations to the team. Under the circum—"

"I am," Billy cut in. "I just felt like coming back. To visit. Have a look around. See who's doing what. Maybe watch the fireworks from a front-row seat."

"Oh, for God's sake, Billy, you'll screw up the whole deal if you don't keep your head down. I suppose you've gone blundering in and demanded the Lambert women turn over that cruddy little cottage to you?"

"Woman," Billy corrected him.

"What?"

"Lambert woman. Singular. The granddaughter. The grandmother's dead. And yes, I did."

"You promised you'd stay away until this whole thing was so well under way that nothing could stop it. Didn't I tell you that vengeance was a damn poor motive for anything? Well, it's an even worse reason to foul up a sweetheart deal like you've got going up there on that island." Glenn Klemchuck's disgust was plain in his voice, eliciting an uncharacteristic need in Billy to defend himself.

"This isn't vengeance, Glenn. This is just taking what's rightfully mine. Now. Instead of waiting for the rest of it to fall into place."

"And the rest of it? Is that still going ahead?"

Billy swallowed. "Yeah." He lit another cigarette he really didn't want.

"Do I hear a shade of doubt?"

"No. No doubt at all."

"And did I just hear you light a smoke?"

"God, you've got good ears!"

"All us gods have good ears. I thought you quit three years ago."

"I did." Billy knew he sounded sullen. Nope, he shouldn't have come back. It was doing bad things to him.

"So you started up again."

"Not . . . really. It's just tonight. I needed one. So I bought a pack."

Glenn's voice was thoughtful. "The granddaughter?"

"Yeah."

"You still got the hots for her, Billy?"

"Hell, no!" The fit of his jeans was none of Glenn's business, and besides, that had been a momentary aberration, nothing more—a reaction to a potent memory brought on by revisiting old haunts. Same as the smoking. He could control them both.

"Don't worry, Glenn," he said. "You'll get your cut."

"I'm not worried about my cut. If I never make another dime off you, I'll have done all right. What I'm worried about, you damn fool, is you."

"Gee, thanks, Mom. G'night."

Billy hung up, cutting off the clearly shouted "Wait!" that came over the phone lines from Phoenix. He didn't want to hear a lecture, and that's what Glenn would try to deliver. Besides, he'd spent the last few hours telling himself exactly what Glenn would have said—that he was a fool to have gone to Oakmount, and an even worse one for crossing the bridge. But, fool or not, he'd done both, and somehow he couldn't find it in himself to regret it.

Both sides of Oakmount had figured too largely in his past, just as they'd figured largely in the lives of so many others. He'd never been able to escape the Oakmounts, no matter where he'd gone or what he'd done. Maybe he'd been drawn back because it was time he figured out, once and for all, how to break free of the past.

The past . . .

Once, the Lamberts had owned the entire island. A few generations back, the first Lambert had acquired most of it under the Homestead Act, and bought the rest when the government of the day was all but giving away land in the Puget Sound area in order to get the place populated and civilized. Judge Lambert's father, grandson of the original settler, had been the one to subdivide the land into nineteen exclusive properties, keeping the original homestead, which comprised the entire southern end of the eight-mile-long Island, for himself. Because he had wanted the right kind of neighbors, he'd sold to only those who could afford the high prices he set, prices which precluded any but the very cream of the buying public.

When it was necessary for an owner to sell, the estate was never advertised, but sold through word-of-mouth. There was a clause in every purchase agreement; if an Oakmount Islander had to sell, he must offer the property first to fellow owners. Only if none of them were able to come up with the assessed market value plus ten percent could the Islander sell to outside interests. Even then, present dwellers had the last say on whether or not to accept the new owner. This kept the Island's population the way the judge's late father had wanted it, comprised of wealthy, respected professionals and businessmen. Some were only summer visitors, others, however, made their homes on the Island, commuting to Seattle, an hour's drive beyond the end of the private bridge linking Oakmount Island with Oakmount Village on the mainland.

The owners were all men who could afford the high upkeep of their private docks, where cabin cruisers rocked in the sheltered waters and float planes nudged the fenders of the wharves. They could also afford the private and exclusive school that educated their children from kindergarten through eighth grade, as well as the guards who sat at the Village end of the bridge twenty-four hours a day, keeping out those who did not belong.

The Village, which had grown up over the years to serve the wealthy landowners across the narrow inlet, had started out as a small logging and fishing community. When the original Lambert had needed lumber to build his house, he financed a man who built a sawmill on the outskirts of town. The mill had prospered, and the town began to grow as more workers were hired. Oakmount Village became a viable entity in its own right.

The Islanders, however, continued to see the Village as there for their use and convenience. Mostly, though, they were too busy with their practices and businesses and other pursuits to think about the Village at all—except, on certain occasions, to wish that Billy Culver lived *there* and not *here*, that the judge had never brought Jenny and her fatherless son into their exclusive midsts.

Billy Culver's father had been a wastrel who stayed around "long enough to provide the sperm," as Jenny was wont to put it years later when it no longer mattered to her. She had been a hardworking woman who tried to provide a good home for her child. She raised him in the housekeeper's cottage on Judge Lambert's property, where he really should never have been raised at all.

That, and the fact that the judge arranged for him to be educated with the children of the landowners, where small class sizes and the very best of teachers ensured an excellent grounding for the students, gave Billy ideas somewhat above his station.

But the children all liked him. Probably, it was said, they liked him because he knew how to find so much trouble for them to get into, although the kids called it "fun."

After all, Oakmount Island had standards. It always had. But, standards or not, Billy did live on the Island, and until the age of thirteen attended Oakmount Academy, getting himself and everyone in his realm in trouble with increasing frequency, but always managing to squeak out of it.

He also remained a straight-A student, even under the exacting standards set by the board of directors of Oakmount Academy. That earned him a lot of forgiveness, as did the fact that he was, after all, polite to adults and well-spoken, with a lot of charm to go with the keen intelligence the teachers kept harping on.

He'd grow up, the adults assured one another, but not without some unease as they noticed how handsome he was becoming, with his sharp, blue eyes, his untamed inky curls, his flashing dimples. Mentally, they gathered their precious, well-bred daughters a little closer and looked forward to the time they'd be sending them back east, or, at the very least, into Seattle to private high schools, where the likes of Billy Culver weren't a threat.

Even after he left the academy and went over the bridge to the Village high school, Billy seemed to be a threat to everyone's daughters, though no one could have said exactly how. He spent all his spare time with Arlene Lambert to the exclusion of other girls.

He just made people uneasy. He had grown too accustomed to being able to charm himself out of trouble. He relied on being smart and athletic to keep him from having to answer for his misdeeds. After all, who was going to throw out the best team player in the school, one who was clearly academic scholarship material as well?

By the time he was halfway through high school, he was not only the star of the basketball team, but captain of the football team as well, and aceing every class to boot. Even when he drank like a fish, and got caught with marijuana, he still got top marks and scored impossible goals.

However, after the judge put the kibosh on his association with Arlene, he also scored all too regularly with the Village girls. He was not safe to have around, and somebody really should take the boy in hand. But who?

The judge did what he could, though that was little. Billy would promise to be good, but he'd be out of sight and acting up the minute the judge's back was turned, which was often. The judge, after all, had court sessions to see to, and that certainly took precedence over the antics of his housekeeper's ill-behaved son. Because of his duties, he was home only on weekends, leaving his granddaughter and his wife on their own.

On a few occasions, his son, George, Arlene's father, came back from wherever it was he spent his time digging for antiquities. But he was much too vague even to be approached by those who concerned themselves that Billy was getting increasingly out of hand. It was all the judge's son could do to reacquaint himself with his only child. He certainly couldn't be expected to pay any attention to the housekeeper's kid.

The trouble was, some of the teachers from Oakmount Academy claimed, that once out of their jurisdiction and into the public high school, Billy fast grew bored. Thanks to his excellent early education, he knew as much, if not more, than many of his teachers over the bridge, and was cocky enough to let them know it every chance he got. There was nothing to challenge him in his new school, nothing to keep his mind busy enough to stay out of trouble.

So he didn't.

Lying there in the motel, Billy remembered how, as he entered his teens, he had discovered that "smart" as in "intelligent" wasn't enough in the affluent community where he lived. Smart had a different meaning, and once he learned that, he could see he was hopelessly outclassed.

To children, money might matter little. To adolescents, it mattered more, and humiliations suffered by a teenager linger on. Billy recalled every bit of that humiliation, every unkind cut, every single time one of his former friends treated him as less than equal, shunned him, even laughed at him when he tried, stupidly, to maintain his friendships with them. Or worse, when they had patronized him, pretended to be his buddy because he was a good source of dope. For a while he'd been taken in. But only for a while.

After school and on weekends, he worked in Hansen's Grocery. He needed the money to help out his mother. But the job left him without much leisure time, the kind of time demanded by girls like Arlene Lambert. Not that Arlene demanded anything of him. Of all the Island kids, she was the one who steadfastly remained his friend, if only in a limited way.

After she graduated from the academy, she pleaded not to be sent away. Her grandparents, always indulgent, agreed reluctantly. With a cautious eye on her and her association with their housekeeper's son, they let her attend the local high school. But suddenly Arlene, like the other Island kids, became very busy with such things as ski weekends in places like Whistler and Mt. Rainier, while he was busy with rotten lettuce leaves in the back room of Hansen's Grocery. Their times together grew less frequent, and more precious to Billy.

Of course, with his looks and personality, he found other friends with no trouble at all. He also learned that "fun" was to be had hanging around with what his mother called "the wrong people"—drinking on the beach after work, burning rubber on the highway outside of town, getting stoned and taking risks. Hell, he'd been taking risks all his life. A few more, with greater potential penalties, were just that much more fun.

Such terms as "wild" and "incorrigible" were soon used to describe Billy Culver, descriptions he heard with a bitter kind of pride. If his new friends were the wrong kind of people, then he was a wrong kind of person too. At least they accepted him. They had the same kind of income he had, the same kind of clothes, the same kind of cars. If only he'd had the sense years before to see that he didn't really fit with the Oakmount Island crowd, he wouldn't have wasted so much time with them.

No. In spite of what his mother said, his new friends were the ones he should be with. The girls he dated were his kind of people.

He knew that it was only a matter of time before he got kicked out of school if he didn't shape up, but he just couldn't find a way to do that. There was too much rage in him burning to get out— especially after that time he'd come home early from work and found the judge humping his mother.

Even now, more than twenty years later, it made him feel sick. Then, it had made him puke. For months after, he would waken at night, the picture imprinted on his mind of the judge's naked backside, white boxer shorts around his knees, and his mother's legs wrapped around that flabby middle, both bodies heaving in an obscene dance. Every time, he threw up. His mother accused him of drinking himself sick.

Sometimes it was true.

His grades, always a source of pride, even when he was raising lots of hell, fell off. He quit the football squad and, because of his drinking, was kicked off the basketball team. The principal despaired and threatened. Then there was the car he and Morry swiped and wrecked. He'd come close to jail that time, getting probation instead, but he didn't really give a damn. The principal had given him a week's suspension the first time he actually came into class drunk. His mother wept. The judge counseled, or tried to, but Billy flung the old man's filthy hand off his shoulder and bolted.

He seemed caught up in a spiral of events that he couldn't escape, and he was heading downhill faster than fast. Finally, the judge refused to permit Arlene to associate with him at all, and Billy got madder and badder until, in the end, it seemed there was no hope for him.

Arlene, of course, paid no more heed to her grandfather's edict than Billy did to his mother's cautioning that if he tried to see her, there'd be trouble. When he looked at her, he ached over how pretty she was with her honey-brown hair hanging in a long, sleek stream down her back, her gray eyes big and full of secrets he wanted to probe. Whenever the two of them could meet secretly, they did. He was careful, though, not to go beyond the kissing she was getting so damned good at, it made it nearly impossible to stop. However, he tried to restrain himself.

Arlie was special. She was sacrosanct. There were plenty of girls over the inlet who were experienced and willing and who didn't have rich families that would kill him if he was discovered making out with their daughters.

He knew he shouldn't have touched her, but her hips had started pumping while he was kissing her. Little sounds had come from the back of her throat, and she'd thrust her body hard against his, rubbing herself on his thigh. So he'd lost control, and let his hand kind of sneak up her leg and then his fingers had found their way inside her panties and through the curly hair there. She'd come in a rush at the first touch of his fingers against her wet flesh. She hadn't known what was happening to her, and had stared at him, shaking and quivering, half laughing, half crying. She whispered his name over and over until the spasms tapered off, leaving her limp and stunned, still staring into his eyes.

And at that precise moment her grandfather had walked in on them where they were curled together on the sun porch in a squeaky swing. They hadn't even known he was back on the Island.

Within the week Arlene was gone from the Island without saying good-bye, and when she came home at Easter, he saw her only from a distance and quickly turned his back.

It hadn't taken the judge's threat to fire Jenny and have her, along with her rotten son, thrown off the

Island to keep Billy from seeking Arlene out. He'd learned his lesson. Arlene Lambert was strictly out of bounds.

The next time he saw her, she poked her cute little nose up into the air and ignored him, walking away, swinging a tennis racquet, accompanied by three friends, two of whom were male and dressed in Brooks Brothers' best . . . and were stupid bastards, every one of them.

He finally got kicked out of school in his senior year, and he told himself and everyone else that he didn't give a damn.

He lost his job in the grocery store shortly after that because he mouthed off at old man Hansen. His head had been as big and as hollow as a pumpkin that day, and Hansen had nattered on too long about all the things he was doing wrong. His mother despaired and he mouthed off at her, too, even though he'd apologized later.

"He'll end up doing time," he heard the judge tell his son, George, home for a brief spell. "And it will either shake him up enough to realize that a boy of his intelligence has better things to do with his life than raise hell, or will turn him into a hardened criminal. At any rate, I've done all I can."

Billy took those words to heart and tried, seriously, to clean up his act. After a few months of no trouble at all, he got up the nerve to ask permission to take Arlene to a dance. The answer wasn't a simple, plain no. The old man got mad enough to turn purple and tell Billy he was a worthless guttersnipe who wasn't fit to put air in his granddaughter's car's tires. He hadn't helped matters by getting mad and telling the judge that he loved Arlene, and someday he'd be as rich as the Lamberts, and when he was, he'd buy up the whole damn Island and log it bald, then he'd take Arlene away.

Though it had been close, the judge hadn't had

his stroke then. It had come nearly six months later. He had it, not in his chambers, where he was supposed to be, but in the subbasement of a posh downtown Seattle hotel, where a secret and high-stakes series of poker games had been taking a large toll of the Lambert finances over the years.

It wasn't learned that the judge had gone deeply into debt to pay for his gambling until George, hastily summoned from his latest dusty pit somewhere in North Africa, came home to take care of things for his helpless and devastated mother. Unable to speak, perhaps unable to hear or see, Judge Lambert was declared non compos mentis. George was appointed his agent, and the big house with all its problems, including Billy and his mother, passed into the safekeeping of the judge's son.

He didn't want the responsibility, didn't know how to look after things, and, many people suspected, simply didn't care—especially in light of what he did in the end.

George was appalled by the huge debt load his father's compulsive and previously unknown gambling had created. He quickly put on the market a huge chunk of the southern end of the Island, to the dismay of the other owners, all of whom were intent on protecting their exclusiveness.

"What about the covenant?" they demanded, and were stunned to learn that the Lamberts, who had inherited the property, not bought it, were not governed by the same compact.

Exclusivity be damned was the way George looked at it. His mother and daughter needed an income that he, as an archaeologist dependent on university grants, was incapable of providing. The sale of the land would see to it that they had what they needed. He sold to the highest bidder and didn't care that it was offshore money.

Then, with the obligations finally met, and little

left of the Lambert estate besides the house and a couple of acres of grounds, George prepared to return to North Africa, where he wouldn't have to deal with things he'd never understood.

Due to the Lamberts' reduced financial status, a housekeeper was a luxury Mrs. Lambert could no longer afford. Much of the house was shut up. She and Arlene lived in three or four rooms on the main floor they could take care of themselves.

Jenny Culver, who had worked for the judge and his wife for fifteen years, reeled with the shock of losing her job, to say nothing of a good friend—and an occasional lover. She genuinely loved the judge, and grieved over his illness probably more than his wife, who remained outraged by his secret gambling. Letitia Lambert knew nothing, of course, of his other secret, and graciously permitted Jenny to continue living in the cottage.

On a hot July morning shortly before George was to depart, one more problem arose. It affected him only peripherally in that good manners dictated he stay another few days. Billy's mother died of an aneurism while scrubbing the floor of a doctor's house on Lombardy Street. Billy, who was greasing a Chevy in Mortimer's Garage on the corner of Short Street and Arbutus Avenue, dimly heard an ambulance go by, but paid it no heed. On Short Street, ambulances and cop cars were commonplace.

When the toe of Mortimer's dirty boot poked at him under the Chevy and Mortimer said, "Hey, Billy, I got bad news for ya," he thought he'd been fired. It wouldn't have surprised him. He'd been fired from six jobs already that year. He rolled out from under the Chevy on the low cart and looked up from under the edge of his dirty cap, waiting for Mortimer's words. "Yer ma just got took to the hospital. They say she's dead."

• • •

He was twenty years old, and he had buried his mother. He was on his own now, a grown man, and he shouldn't be hiding in a secret, grassy hollow between three old rhododendron bushes, crying like a little boy. And he wouldn't be. In just a minute he'd stop. He'd pick himself up out of the grass and march out of the hidey-hole that had been his since he was a kid of seven. Then he'd pack his things and go.

George Lambert had made it clear that his tenure in the cottage was over. If he wanted to stay in the area, he was going to have to find a place off the Island—in the Village with his own kind. George hadn't said it, but the message had been implicit. He was to go away, and stay away, from the estate where he'd lived since the age of five but had never truly belonged. And, of course, from George's daughter, Arlene.

He'd stood alone and thrown a clod of dirt on a pale brown box deep in a hole in the ground of Oakmount Village Cemetery, a hole in the ground bought and paid for by Lambert money. George didn't seem to find it strange that his generosity in insisting the family take care of funeral arrangements, "because your mother was a member of my parents' household," didn't extend to permitting her son to continue living in the only home he remembered until he could find something else. No. Billy was to be out of there by morning. Once Jenny Culver was buried, the Lamberts' responsibility toward her only child was over.

Billy had wondered if George knew just how much a member of his parents'—at least his father's—household Jenny had been, but only shrugged. The judge was a vegetable, Billy's mother was dead, and

Arlene wasn't his friend anymore. What did it matter where he went? He only knew it wasn't going to be anywhere near Oakmount—Village or Island.

Funeral over, he'd turned and walked away. He walked past the few people who were standing near him but not with him—past George Lambert and his delicate, wispy mother, past the unexpected and stolid figure of Mortimer from the garage, past the robed minister and some old ladies from the church his mother had attended infrequently, and past Miss Quail, his mother's best friend, whom he'd known most of his life. He went past without looking at any of them, just as he went past the pale, suddenly blurred shape that he knew was Arlene. He saw her hand reach out to him, but pretended he did not. He knew it fell helplessly to her side as he turned away, his long legs striding out of the cemetery, through the Village, and back over the bridge to the Island.

He ran into the woods behind the cottage, woods recently sold to some stranger. He didn't care that he was trespassing. He'd known these trails since his early childhood. He knew them better than anybody.

He had run for miles along secret paths, and then along no path at all, forging his own, ripping from his neck the narrow tie Mr. Lambert had given him to wear, letting it fall from his hand when it tangled on a bush. The dark suit his mother had saved up to buy for him for the high school graduation he hadn't achieved was too tight across the shoulders, the sleeves were too short. The pants pinched his crotch, but he continued to run until he could run no more and then he had walked.

When he came back, at last, to the cottage, its emptiness haunted him, echoing in his head, and he ripped the suit from his body, sending it flying across the room to drape over the immaculate hearth of the stone fireplace. He wanted to stuff it into the grate and set it alight, but did not. Tugging on a pair of jogging shorts, he loped from the house, seeking solace in the one place he knew he might find it.

But even there, in his secret place, no solace to be found as he knelt, face buried in his hands, weeping.

Not until Arlene arrived and knelt before him. Sliding her strong young arms around his bare, heaving back, she drew his face to her firm breasts, and rocked him as he wept.

FOUR

"Go away!" he told her, clinging to her with all his might. "I don't want you here!"

"I know, I know," she whispered, her breath warm against his temple. "I'll go in a minute. When you don't need me anymore."

"I don't need you now!" His face remained hidden against her breasts. He tried to stop crying, but the tears kept on coming from some bottomless well deep inside him. He didn't know there were that many tears in one person, that depth of desolation.

He had no one, for the first time in his life, and facing it tore him up.

"I don't need anyone," he said, as much for his own information as for hers.

"I know," she said again. "But I need to be with you, Billy. I'm sad too. I loved your mother. And I love you. That's why I made them let me come home for her funeral." He felt her tears splattering on his bare shoulder. He held her tightly, giving comfort as well as taking it. This was Arlie, and in spite of everything he'd tried to tell himself, she was his friend. She was also right; he needed her. After a while her tears stopped, as did his.

"Do they know you're here? I mean now, with me?" he asked when he thought he'd be able to trust his voice again. It came out thick and not nearly as firm as he'd have liked, but Arlie didn't seem to notice. At least she didn't laugh at him.

"No. They think I'm in my room. I climbed into the maple tree and down. I hated to think of you being alone, today of all days. When I couldn't find you at the cottage, just your suit, I knew you'd be here."

The silence between them went on and on until he said huskily, "I haven't been here for a long time."

"I know. After they said I couldn't see you anymore and sent me away to school, I used to come here whenever I got to return home, hoping you'd be here. You never were."

"No."

There was silence again as they listened to each other breathe until he said, "I thought you'd decided you didn't want to see me anymore—that I'd scared you, or hurt you or something. I thought maybe the embarrassment of your grandpa catching us like that had been too much for you, and that was why you hadn't even said good-bye."

She shook her head. "Uh-uh. And I wasn't embarrassed."

That, he knew, was a lie. She'd been mortified, going white, then red, then white again as the judge first stared at them in disbelieving horror, then bellowed at Billy. He'd snatched his hand out from under her skirt and wiped it unobtrusively on the leg of his jeans, wondering if the old man could smell the sex of her as strongly as he could. He'd been embarrassed too, and sick with shame.

"I wanted to say good-bye to you, Billy, but they kept watching me. They were afraid we'd sneak away together and finish what we'd started." She ducked her head down to peer into his eyes, looking at him shyly. "I would have if I could have."

He lifted his head and stared at her. "Would have what?" *Said good-bye, or . . .*

"Finished what we started."

"Like hell!" he barked. "Or if you had, you'd have finished it on your own. I wouldn't have done more than what I did do, Arlene, and I shouldn't have done that much. I knew it, even if you didn't."

She shifted in his embrace and laid her head against the top of his. "Why not?"

"Because it wouldn't have been right. You're— who you are. And I'm . . . well, I'm your house-keeper's son. They did the best thing, sending you away, keeping us apart."

"No, they did not! We were supposed to be friends forever, Billy. We promised each other, remember? We didn't have to let them change that. We could have seen each other without them know-ing—like we did before, when you got drunk that time and Grandpa said I couldn't talk to you anymore."

"No." He shook his head, lifted it slightly, and wiped his face against the shoulder of her pale yel-low dress, then sniffed long and wetly. He sighed. He should have felt ashamed that he didn't have a handkerchief, but he didn't. After letting Arlie see him blubbering like that, he guessed he didn't have much shame left. Or much pride.

"I didn't want to get you in trouble. And I would have. I was a bad influence on you. You're not the same as me, Arlene. Your life won't be the same as mine. You'll go to college, meet someone, get mar-ried, and have clean, pink babies that will come here and play on the sand, like you used to."

And I couldn't bear to be here to see it.

"Like we used to do."

He thought about that. "I was never a clean, pink baby," he said tiredly after several moments had passed. "I was a tough, dirty little boy."

"I loved you anyway, and you were never dirty for long. Not once your mom caught you." She laughed, a small tinkle of sound that filled his soul with peace for the moment. His smile was small, but it was there, curving against the fabric of her cotton dress. He lifted his head, wishing he knew how to thank her for making him smile. He'd thought he'd forgotten how, the past three days.

"I can remember you hollering when she washed your ears," Arlene said.

"Yeah. She always pulled them."

She tugged gently on one of his ears. "So, I guess you weren't so tough, then."

"No. Maybe not then. But I am now. Now I'm what they all say."

"And what's that?" She stroked his cheek.

"A tough punk. Useless. Going nowhere. A high school dropout with grease under my nails, dirt ground right into my hands. I shouldn't even be touching your clothes. I'll probably leave stains."

"It doesn't matter to me. I love you, Billy. I always have."

Her low-voiced, fierce words smacked into his chest like the time Kelly Krantz had swung a tire iron at him and connected. He drew in a long breath and let it out in a gusty sigh as he shook his head. "No, you don't, Arlene. I'm not the kind of guy a girl like you can love."

"Why not?"

God, she was so innocent, so pretty, so tempting. "I'll . . . never be clean enough for you."

Her cheeks flared with color as she said, "That's stupid! And who are you to say that I don't love you? You don't know how I feel! You can't get inside me and feel the way I do! I've missed you, all this time I've been away. I don't care what your nails look like! It's what you are, who you are, that matters. And you're the boy—the man—I love." She lifted one of his hands and brushed her mouth over the large, rough knuckles, then turned it and pressed a kiss into the callused palm.

"Don't!" he said gruffly, snatching his hand away, pressing it to his thigh, scrubbing it against the hair-rough skin, trying to erase the soft feel of her lips.

"Billy . . . it was good, that day, what you did to me."

"Stop it!" He groaned, aching for the feel of her lips against his skin again. "It was all wrong. It should never have happened. You were just a kid."

Shyly, she put her hands around his face, her gentle, delicate fingers brushing the skin under his ears, her thumbs making tiny, quivering arcs against the salty stains beneath his eyes. "I'm not a kid now," she said, leaning back from him. "I'm a woman, Billy. I'm seventeen, nearly eighteen. And I love you."

God, she had him shaking as if he were freezing to death. It was all he could do to keep his teeth from chattering, he was shaking so hard. "No, Arlene. You're not a woman. Not yet. But I'm a man." He cleared his throat of the lump that rose into it. "A man on my own."

"What are you going to do now, Billy? My dad says he asked you to . . . to vacate the cottage. I begged him to let you stay, but he won't. Will you—will you stay in Oakmount?" Her voice quivered. Her eyes filled with a sheen of tears.

He didn't need that. It would weaken him when he needed most of all to be strong. He flopped down and lay flat on his back, refusing to look at her. He stared up at the tall cedars that shaded their rhododendron nook. They used to pretend to fly in their imaginary spaceship there. What was it he'd called himself? Conquering Hero, Master of the Spaceways, Commander of the Ship. Hell, look at him now. He commanded nothing. He was master of nothing, not even his own fate. And when it came to conquering, he was lucky he'd been able to vanquish his weeping.

"No. I don't belong here. I'll pack my stuff tonight and get out of the cottage."

He swallowed hard and added, "But I don't know what to do . . . with her things." He felt tears well up in his eyes again and hated them, hated her for being there to see them. How could he hate someone he loved so much? He flung his arm over his eyes.

"I'll help you pack them up, and you don't have to leave the cottage today," she cried. "You have one more night. Stay, Billy!"

"I don't want to stay, Arlie. There's nothing here for me."

"What about me?" she asked in a tiny voice.

Again he refused to look at her. "What about you?"

"I mean . . . I'll feel bad if you leave."

He remembered the guys and their tennis racquets. "Not for long," he said.

"Forever. I promise you that." Impulsively, she leaned over him, snatched his arm down and kissed his damp eyes. Then emboldened by his muffled gasp and involuntary shudder, she placed her lips over his and kissed him.

He quivered again at the sweet contact of her lips. She parted hers experimentally against his, and the tiny, explorative tip of her tongue brushed against him.

"Don't!" He thrust her back, his fingertips biting into her shoulders. Then he let her go, and rolled away from her, too stiff in the front of his shorts to risk standing.

"Why? It was just a kiss, Billy. I like kissing you. Remember when you taught me how?" She got up and came around to lie beside him. Propping herself on an elbow, she slid the fingers of one hand behind his neck and leaned against him, putting her mouth to his once more. This time, she slid her tongue between his lips, but he kept his teeth clenched to form an impassible barrier.

"Kiss me back, Billy," she begged, but he sat up abruptly and pushed her away again. She sat back on her haunches, her yellow dress spilling out around her, making her look like a daffodil in the green grass. She lifted her hands to his face again.

He grew harder just looking at her, remembering the feel of her tongue against his lips. He dragged her hands down and placed them on her lap. Sinking back himself, he lifted one knee so she couldn't see what had happened to his body.

"Arlene, we're beyond that kind of kissing and fooling around now. We aren't kids experimenting with each other."

"We weren't kids when you taught me to use my tongue," she said. "I was fifteen. You were seventeen."

"Nearly eighteen," he said in a strangled tone. "Old enough to know better." He was rigid, harder than he'd ever been in his life, remembering that first day he'd ever kissed her, the magic of her velvety mouth, her sweet lack of experience, her tentative little forays with her tongue when he asked her for it. "And you damned well were a kid."

She got to her feet and circled around to stand in front of him. "And now I'm the one who's nearly eighteen."

"That's right," he said harshly, leaping up and turning his back on her. "Nearly eighteen and also old enough to know better. Old enough to know what a little tongue can do to make a kiss feel better. Old enough to know what it does to me to feel your tongue in my mouth," he added, turning to face her again, catching her upper arms in his hands, shaking her. She stared up at him, her gray eyes wide and puzzled.

"Doesn't it matter to you that I love you? Don't you love me even a little bit anymore, Billy?"

"I . . . dammit, of course I do. But that doesn't mean I'm going to take advantage of what you're offering, whether you know you're offering it or not!"

"I know what I'm offering. Don't forget, if you knew what you were doing when you were nearly eighteen, so do I, now that I'm that age." All at once her eyes filled with tears, and she leaned against his chest, sobbing, "You're going away, Billy! I know I can't stop you, but I don't want to lose you! It was bad enough not being able to see you except in passing, or when I sneaked away. But now you'll be gone forever, and I'll never see you again. I love you so much I don't know what to do, and I want you to kiss me good-bye as if you really do love me like you say!"

With a groan that might have been a disguised sob, he dragged her into a full embrace, spreading his legs to pull her between his thighs. Need exploded in his body, and his lips forced hers open to admit the full strength of his plunging tongue.

She made a soft sound of happiness and wound her arms around his neck, going limp in his embrace, heavier and heavier, until the weight of her inert body pulled him to the ground with her. She slid one leg over his, her bare heel caressing the skin of his calf. So rapidly and intensely did desire flare between them that he had no chance of controlling it.

It burned like a brilliant flame, scorching him, heating his skin, hurrying his hands as he ran them down her sides to her waist, then back up to cup her small, hard breasts and finger the taut nipples jutting against the cloth of her dress. She wore no bra. His head spun, knowing how close to bare her breasts were.

She made that soft, welcoming sound again and moved against him, nibbling at his neck and shoulder until his body hummed with need. She twisted in his arms and reached behind her. Then the top of her dress was suddenly loose, falling from her shoulders, baring her breasts to his greedy mouth. As he sucked, he slid his hands to the hem of her dress, then under it to the elastic of her fine-textured bikini panties. Reaching inside, he stroked her. Then as she lifted her hips in silent invitation, he tugged her panties down and cast them away.

He had never felt skin so smooth as that of her inner thighs, nor a need so great as the one driving him to feel that skin against his own. She shifted as he stroked her thighs, then moaned when his fingers slid into her most private recess. She was wet and pulsating as she surged against his probing fingers, crying out with little sounds of encouragement and want. She shuddered finally, as she had the other time, a deep, uncontrollable spasm that made her voice go high and cracked as she called his name. Then she stared at him with stunned, half-vacant eyes.

"Oh, Billy! I love you!" She gasped, reaching down to touch his erection through the cloth of his shorts. It was more than he could bear. With an inarticulate grunt he heaved himself up and sideways, stripping off the single garment he wore. Then he was over her, between her thighs, his head reared back, gasping as he entered her.

He felt the dam of her hymen give before his frenzied, unstoppable onslaught, felt her first startled spasm of pain, and held her tightly as she tried to get away from it, but not from him. He heard her cry out, sharply, shrilly, and covered her mouth with his own. She still sobbed, but silently, as he continued to hurt her. He wanted to stop, but he could not. Nothing on earth could have stopped the pistoning of his flesh as it slid in and out of hers. On and on it went. He was driven by a force he didn't comprehend, plunging into her deeper and deeper, harder and harder, her hips held tightly in his hands, lifting her high off the ground so that he could pound her down with each thrust.

He was weeping himself as he came, great spurts of fluid that seemed to issue from the very depths of him, deep as the well of tears he had discovered within himself. He had never come like that before, as if it would never end, and even before it was finished, he was aware that her thighs had lifted high of their own volition, quivering with ungovernable spasms as she clamped unseen muscles tightly around his flesh, milking him. Her knees bent, her legs locked around him, she rode a wave of her own. She was still sobbing after it was all over, but quietly now, with a combination of the crazy joy and despair that closely echoed his own.

"Billy . . . please don't go," she whispered moments later when he stirred and lifted himself off her. "Don't leave me. Love me like that again."

"I can't, Arlie. Never, never again."

"But, Billy, why?" Her fingers clung to him as he rolled away from her, unable to meet her eyes. He shook them off, got to his feet, and turned his back as he pulled his shorts on, listening to the soft sounds of her crying.

She was still lying on the grass, her face buried in her arms. Her yellow dress was rucked up around her middle, her bare buttocks gleaming like twin pale melons, her thighs spread apart. Billy thought of pulling her dress down. He thought of giving her back her panties and telling her to get dressed. He thought of lying down beside her and taking her in his arms, trying to make her understand why he had to leave. He thought of staying, too, and watching her continue to grow up and marry someone her father and grandparents would like, and knew he had no choices left.

Without a word he turned and crept out from behind the rhododendron bushes, his feet, in leaving, as silent as hers had been arriving.

Half an hour later he drove off the Island, still smelling her scent with every breath he took, and hating himself for what he had done. He'd taken her virginity. No matter that she'd given it willingly. He'd been the one who knew the score. He should have found a way to make her stop, and to stop himself. And he hadn't.

If the judge could have known, his hatred for his granddaughter's defiler wouldn't have begun to compete with Billy's self-loathing as he drove through Oakmount Village, stopped at Mortimer's and got what pay was owed to him, then continued on his way. He didn't know where he was going or what he was going to do. He knew only that wherever it was, it would be as far from Oakmount Island, and Arlene Lambert, as this old car would take him.

It took him as far as Phoenix.

And now he was back. Now he had seen Arlie again. And nothing tasted right anymore, not even the sweetness of revenge.

Billy wadded the pillow under his head and waited until light showed around the sides of the drapes. Then he got up and showered again before going out to jog his usual four miles.

When he got back, his message light was blinking. He called the desk.

"You gotta tell people, Billy, that this ain't no big city hotel. You don't have night clerks or nothing like that. Whatcha got is me, and I like to sleep in of a morning."

"You sound wide awake now, Elmer, so how about giving me my message?"

"Messages," grumbled Elmer. "Three of 'em. Two from some guy named Glenn, to call him at once, and one from some woman. Uh . . . Mavis."

Billy's brows drew together in a quick frown. *Mavis?* Heart suddenly thudding hard, he said, "Right. Got it." He ended the call and dialed again quickly.

"Mavis? What's wrong?"

"Nothing, Mr. Culver. Or, not much. Just, I want to go back east for a couple of weeks and wondered if you planned to come home any time soon. My father's getting out of jail and I'd kind of like to be there. For my mother, as much as for him. I asked Mr. Klemchuck, and he said you'd be out of town indefinitely. You didn't tell me you were going any farther than Portland, Mr. Culver." Her voice became accusing. "You didn't tell Holly neither."

"I know, guilty on all counts, and apologies all around. It was a spur-of-the-moment decision. Is Holly up yet?"

"Right here, hanging on to my elbow, waiting to talk to you."

Billy smiled, focusing all his attention on the phone. "Hi, honey bunch. I bought you a pink scarf, just like I promised."

"That's nice. Is it silk?"

"Sure is. Hey, you don't sound real happy. You okay?"

"Yes, but . . . when you coming home?"

"I'm . . . I'm not certain, baby. Soon, I hope."

"It better be. Mavis really does need to go and see her mom and dad, and I'm not staying with Uncle Glenn again. He talks down to me. He's got the weird idea that eight is still a baby."

"Yeah, I know. A lot of adults have that problem. It doesn't mean they're stupid or insensitive, just that they don't know how things really are with you."

"I know, but that doesn't mean I have to like it. So what are we going to do? This is a situation that must be resolved. And soon."

Billy blinked and shook his head. Sometimes that little girl of his took even his breath away with her vocabulary, and he was used to it. He thought briefly—very briefly—of calling Holly's mother. But no. Sherril's career as an actress didn't permit much time for mothering. Besides, they all agreed that it was bad for the ingenue image she tried to project.

He listened to his daughter's impatient breathing as she waited, then made one of his lightning decisions.

"Listen, sweet-chops, pack a bag. No, on second thought, don't. Just put on a pair of jeans, your sneakers, not sandals, and socks—don't forget socks—and bring the jacket of your ski suit. I'm gonna get Mavis to put you on a plane. We'll buy more warm clothes when you get here."

"Daddy, are you in *Alaska*?"

He laughed. "Nope. Next best thing, though, or almost. I'm in Washington—the state, that is—and you're going to join me. Like it?"

"Love it. Will it snow? For how long?"

He laughed. "It might snow. Damn sure is cold enough, but right now it's raining." As to how long he'd be there, well, that he had to think about. "I don't know, sweet-pops."

"Doesn't matter. What plane is Mave going to put me on?"

"Let me talk to her, okay?"

After the obligatory squawk about school and dancing lessons, Mavis agreed to get her young charge on the first flight to Seattle.

An hour later, Billy headed out for the airport. With a wave to Elmer, he screeched his brand-new, very expensive tires and laid rubber halfway down the block.

Throwing back his head, he laughed aloud as he sped through town.

"Oh, yes!" he shouted. "This is gonna be fun!"

He wondered if Oakmount Academy would ever be the same again after its second Culver kid had done her thing.

Arlene shoved her hair back from her face and leapt down from the bank onto a silver beach log, then to the sand. Coarse grass dragged at the legs of her jeans and she pulled free, landing with a skid near the water's edge. It was a beautiful sunny morning—one of those deceptively springlike January days that fooled even the primroses in the garden, all of which had bloomed in response.

"Hello."

The voice startled Arlene, and she turned, coming to a halt as she spotted the little girl sitting hunched on a log, her hands between her knees, her feet tight together, her taffy-colored hair streaming out from under the rolled edge of a ski hat to bracket her cherubic face. What was a stray six-year-old doing here on a Saturday morning, she wondered. "Hi, there," she said, "are you lost?"

"Oh, no." The little girl sat erect. "I know exactly where I am in relation to where I came from. I have a built-in sense of direction."

Arlene smiled and moved her estimate of the child's age upward by several years—except that she was so *small* . . . for thirty-five! "What are you doing here?"

"Waiting for it to snow."

Arlene sat on the log beside the child. "It might

not, you know, at least not today, or even this week.
You could have a long wait."

"Maybe, but I'm patient. My dad says that's a
virtue, but I'm not so sure. It seems to me impetuous people like he is get more done in less time
because they don't wait around to think it over first.
They just do it. Which are you?"

Arlene was fascinated and confused. "Which . . .
what?"

"Impetuous or plodding." The small nose wrinkled.

"I suppose I'm more plodding than impetuous,
but I prefer to call it prudent or cautious."

"Hmm. Yes. Both good words. I'll tell my dad
that I like prudent better than plodding."

She might have asked any other child, Who is
your dad. But she felt compelled to ask this child,
with her quick mind and impressive vocabulary,
"Who are you?"

"I'm Holly Culver. My dad is Billy Culver. We live
in a cottage about a mile from here, that way."

Her sense of direction was just fine, Arlene
noticed as she swallowed a quick roughness in her
throat. Billy was married, and the father of a little
girl? *Then why did he kiss me like that three days ago?*
The question popped into her mind, startling her
with its clarity, and she answered it with equal
swiftness. *Because Billy does what he pleases and clearly,
at that moment, it pleased him to kiss the living daylights
out of me. It meant nothing, of course. To him or to me.*

She placed her attention on the child again.
"Hello, Holly Culver. I'm Arlene Lambert."

"Yes. I thought you must be. May I call you
Arlene?"

She smiled. "Yes, of course."

"Thanks. My dad was pretty sure you'd say that,
but he said I should ask. Some grown-ups don't like
to be called by their first names. At least not by
eight-year-olds." Again, that delicate little nose

wrinkled. "Like *Uncle* Glenn. I have to call him that, and I feel really silly because it makes people ask if he's my dad's brother or my mom's and I have to say that he's neither. They ask because he doesn't look at all like my dad, and they're usually trying to find out who my mother is because Daddy and I refuse to discuss that with people." A gamine grin lit up her face. "They think they're being subtle."

"I see. Well, I won't ask."

"Good. Do you really think it won't snow today?"

Arlene nodded. "I really believe that. Quite strongly, in fact. Why do you want it to snow?"

"I'm from Phoenix, and we get snow only in the mountains."

"Of course. That explains it." It also explained the tanned face and sun-bleached tips on Holly's hair.

"Aren't you cold?" the little girl asked. "I mean, you're not even wearing a jacket."

"No." Arlene frowned. Holly's lips were nearly blue. "But you are, aren't you."

Holly nodded. "Freezing. I'm not acclimatized, you see."

Arlene stood and brushed the sand off her bottom. "I don't suppose you'd like to walk with me? I'm only going around the beach a bit, but it would help you keep warm."

"No. Another time, though. I think I'll wait and see what happens here." Holly seemed quite content to continue sitting, practicing her patience in spite of the weather advisory and the cold she was feeling.

What a young-old little person Billy's child was, Arlene mused. "Well, that's fine, but be careful you don't sit too long and get really chilled, won't you? Good-bye, Holly. I'm glad we met."

And she was, Arlene realized as she walked back toward the house half an hour later. After the initial shock of learning that Billy had a child, she'd realized that she shouldn't have been surprised. Why wouldn't he have married? The surprise would have been if he had not. Clearly, though, from what his daughter said, he and his wife did not live together. She wondered why the woman's identity was a secret.

She paused, gazing along the beach at the small, patient figure who remained huddled on the log, waiting for snow. "Impetuous?" she said aloud, approaching the steps that led up from the beach. "Acclimatize?" She laughed. That was some little girl Billy Culver had produced with that unknown woman eight years ago.

"Hi, Arlie, what's the joke?"

Her head jerked up and she met Billy's blue gaze. Her heart gave one good, solid thud and then settled down to a slightly syncopated rhythm. "Good morning," she managed to say quite coolly. She didn't explain the joke because he spoke up again, quickly.

"Did you happen to see a little fair-haired girl with blue eyes anywhere around? I guess I slept in, and she's skipped out on me without breakfast."

"She's along that way, waiting for snow."

"Damn," he said. "On a day like this?"

Arlene laughed softly again, wondering why she didn't feel more awkward with him. Maybe because she was fully dressed and it was broad daylight and she'd had several days to get used to the idea that Billy was back. This was the first time she'd seen him since the night when he'd kissed her and left her with what sounded like a threat. "She says she's patient."

He nodded. "She is."

"She also suggested you'd called her plodding because of it." There was a faint note of disapproval in her tone.

His brows rose. "I never did! Plodding? God,

she's anything but. Except she never acts irrationally. She does think things through. Her thought processes, however, are faster than most computers." He pulled a face. "Poor little kid's a genius."

Arlene wasn't surprised. It explained the adult way the child had of talking. She probably thought like an adult. "It doesn't seem to bother her," she said. "Anyway, she's now armed with the words *prudent* and *cautious* as alternatives to *plodding*. She says she likes them better."

"You gave them to her." It wasn't a question, and his smile was slow, sweet, and warming. She backed away from it quickly, making a big circle around him as she headed up the stairs to the lawn.

"Thanks, Arlie," he called after her, but she didn't reply, jogging the rest of the way home.

Arlene suppressed a sigh when the knock came on the door that evening just before nine. She had told Sam she couldn't see him tonight, that she had a headache and was going to bed early. Clearly he had decided she needed to be "checked on." Sam was like that, and it irked her. He insisted on maintaining their friendship even though the engagement was off, and kept pressing for a reinstatement, using anything he could think of. He'd probably decided she had a headache because she was lonely or something.

It was not, however, Sam at the door. It was Billy and Holly.

"Hi," they said together.

"May we come in?" Holly asked.

Arlene stepped back, smiling at the little girl. She'd left the ski hat at home, but was wearing the jacket again, and mittens. "Still feeling the cold?"

"Yes" came the fervent, dual reply as Billy shut the door.

"Isn't the cottage warm enough?"

"Oh, that's not the problem. I mean, we're not here because we're cold," said Holly. "Our cable isn't hooked up yet and we have to watch *The Great Divide*. We do it together if we can, and separately if we have to, but every week we watch it. That way we can be a family, you see. Sherril has it right in her contract that she gets to say, somewhere in the show, 'Good night, baby.' " Holly grinned as she unzipped her jacket. "That's me."

Arlene's gaze lifted to Billy's face. He shrugged and nodded. "That's her."

"Sherril McGee is Holly's mother?" Sherril McGee was a teenager! How could she have an eight-year-old daughter?

"Yup."

She swallowed, still staring at Billy. "And your wife."

He shook his head. "Not anymore," he said softly, touching her cheek as he had that first night. "Now it's just Holly and me."

"Oh." The word was a soft breath of air. Something pulsed between them, not really a thought, not really an emotion, but whatever it was, it was nearly tangible. Arlene swallowed, tried to look away, but could not. Billy looked down for an instant, but, as if compelled, his gaze returned to hers, searching, questioning . . .

How long they might have gone on staring at each other like idiots she couldn't have said, but luckily, Billy's daughter knew what was important. "Could we, Arlene? Please? It's nearly nine and I don't want to miss any of it. We get to be a real family only once a week."

She jerked her gaze from Billy's and nodded her head. "Of course," she said, taking Holly's hand. "Come right in. Far be it from me to keep a family apart."

FIVE

"You think I'm a cradle snatcher, don't you?" The quiet, amused voice in her ear stiffened Arlene's erect back even more than it had been. With his hands on her shoulders, Billy pulled her back against the sofa cushions, getting much too close. Shrugging his hands off, she sat forward to evade the puff of warm air from his lips as he spoke again. "Well, don't you?"

Twisting her head around, she looked up at him. "What makes you say that?" Dammit, he was right. Why did Billy always have to be so right about her? She'd been wondering how old he'd been when he married that . . . child . . . over there on the screen. And how old the girl had been. No answer she came up with made the least bit of sense. And thinking about it sent a roiling, burning ache through her insides.

He stood behind her, leaning his arms on the high back of the couch, his eyes full of laughing mischief. "You're sitting there, ramrod straight, like your prim, disapproving old grandma Letitia, Arlie." He ran the tip of a finger from midway down her spine up to her nape. "Come on, loosen up. I like you best when you look like my girl."

Her spine softened momentarily at his touch, then she flinched away from him. "I'm not a girl, yours or otherwise, so you can forget about flirting with me."

"Was I flirting?" he asked innocently.

"You know you were." *And I was responding, like Pavlov's dog, dammit!*

"Well, can you blame me? I came to visit, and you've hardly said two words to me since we got here. Are you mad at me for having married Sherril?"

"I thought you came to watch television."

"We are watching, but I can talk at the same time, can't I?" As the silence lengthened, he got tired of waiting for a reply to his question. "Well? Are you? Mad, I mean."

He wasn't sure why it was so important to know how she felt. It wasn't as if her feelings mattered, one way or another. But dammit, he wanted to know. His frustration grew in proportion to the time she took considering her response. Hell, did she have to *think* about how she felt? He didn't, so why did she?

"No, I'm not mad," she said finally. "Not exactly. Disturbed, maybe, for her sake, considering how young she must have been, but . . . well, it's none of my business who you married and what age she was when you did it, so what reason would I have to be mad?"

His scowl told Arlene he was disappointed by her reasoned reply. It drew his dark brows together into a black slash and shaded his blue eyes. That was good. She wanted him to think she was completely indifferent to him and what he'd done with his life. She wished it weren't a pose.

"In other words," he said, "what I did—my entire life away from here—means nothing to you? You're not curious?" He told himself again it shouldn't matter so much. But what the hell. He'd been telling himself stuff about Arlene all his life and hadn't listened worth a damn anytime before. Why did he expect it to be different now? Restlessly, he stood erect and moved away before something drew him back to her side. Maybe her quiet words.

"When you left, we both went on to other things. Other people. That's the way life is. So what's to be curious about?" It was wiser to keep him and his past in a little box with the lid tightly closed. "Or angry?"

With her lips taut, she turned again to face the television . . . and the child-woman Billy had married. Suddenly she was overwhelmed by the anger she'd denied feeling, and a sense of betrayal, a hurt bigger than she thought she could stand without screaming. Only years of practicing control kept her from showing what she felt, but it roiled in her belly like a poison.

"But . . . what if I tell you all about it anyway?"

"Suit yourself," she said.

"What's your problem? Afraid to hear about it? Think you might get jealous?"

She shot him a dirty look. "Why should I? I've been over my childish infatuation with you for a long, long time."

"Then why not let me tell you about Sherril?"

"I wasn't aware I was stopping you."

"Your attitude's making it difficult, and dammit, I want to tell you," he insisted.

She gave in with a shrug. "Okay, okay. Like I said, please yourself, Billy."

"Why not? I always do." He grinned unpleasantly. "And I pleased you a time or two."

"You aren't pleasing me now." Her response was tart.

He glared at her as angrily. "No, I guess I'm not—Letitia—but give me half a chance, and I will."

She bristled. "Keep your arrogance for those who'll appreciate it!" she said too loudly, then glanced guiltily at Holly, who appeared oblivious to the two adults.

"I'm sorry," Billy said. "I'm being a jerk, aren't I?"

"As a matter of fact . . ." She let her reply trail away, then, a second later, found herself reluctantly responding to Billy's irresistible smile. Her tension suddenly eased away, leaving a void where emotion had burned. But she was terrified a different set of feelings might too easily take their place.

Don't be stupid, she scolded herself, forcing her gaze from his. *Those feelings must be left in the past!*

Billy felt shut out when she lowered her gaze. He tilted her face back up, his hand cradling her jaw, his entire body aware of the silk of her skin, the delicacy of her bones. He looked at her for a long, quiet moment, his smile gone. "You know, I haven't always been able to please myself. There was a time when I was forced to do something that went against my every instinct."

Something in his eyes and his low-pitched voice compelled her to keep looking at him even when she wanted to turn away. Once more, that deep, throbbing sensation began inside her. Once more, the silent chanting began, pulsing through her blood. *Billy, Billy, Billy . . .*

"I didn't want to leave you, Arlie," he said softly. "And I didn't want to stay away all those years. I just didn't see that there was anything to come back for."

She swallowed before she could speak. Tears were too close to the surface, along with other things that must remain buried. "There . . . wasn't," she murmured.

"Wasn't there?" It was a definite challenge.

Pretending to misunderstand, she said, "Oh, yes, your cottage, of course."

"Yeah." After a moment he took his hand off her

face, shoved himself upright and walked around the end of the couch. He sat down too close, facing her, bending one leg so his knee brushed her thigh. His elbow was on the back of the sofa, his fist under his temple as he regarded her solemnly. "But I didn't know about the cottage then. It was you I found hard to stay away from. I missed you, Arlie, for a long time. Thought about you. Wondered about you."

"I wondered about you too, Billy," she said as lightly as she could. "It was only natural that we'd be in each other's thoughts once in a while. We'd been friends all our lives."

"More than friends. And you were in my thoughts more than once in a while." He hesitated, looked troubled. "Especially when I remembered what happened there at the end."

"Don't!" Though her voice was low, its tone was sharp, almost angry. "Can't you forget that part of our relationship? It's all in the past. Like I said, we both met other people, found lives apart from each other."

"Yes, we did, but for me there were a lot of lonely years, a long time of having no one I really belonged to. You, at least, still had your grandparents, your father, your friends, other people you'd known all your life. When I got thrown out of here, I had to . . . start fresh. Make it on my own."

She sighed sharply, thinking about the things he didn't know, thinking about loneliness, and having to do things on her own. He didn't know the half of it. But all she said was "All right. The Lamberts treated you poorly. I know, and I'm sorry my father made you unwelcome here."

Her eyes showed her distress, and Billy would have hushed her, but she rushed on, brushing aside the hand he raised to touch her lips. "Remember, he didn't know then any more than I did that you had a right to stay. He did what he thought was best, Billy. He had a teenaged daughter he believed needed protection. Besides, who are you to complain? You left the area of your own volition. You said there was nothing left here for you, on the Island or in the Village. I assumed that meant me too. For a while it hurt! But I got over it." *When worse disasters showed me what pain really meant.*

He took her left hand, curled her fingers into her palm, and smoothed their backs with his thumb. Sensations and emotion tangled and coiled within her. Oh, God, what was wrong with her? How could she allow this to be happening to her? How could she permit herself to sit and feel the things she was feeling? The answer was, she could not. Not with Billy Culver. She pulled her hand free and locked it with her other on her lap.

As if only now becoming aware of her discomfort, he moved away from her on the couch. "We got off the subject somehow. I was telling you about when I met Sherril. I was twenty-one and she was a pretty little kid of eleven or so." A chuckle escaped him at the sudden flare of shock in her eyes. "No, no! Hey, come on! You really think I'm such a louse?"

She knew her cheeks were pink. Because, for a second, she *had* wondered. Sort of. Just a fleeting question. "Of course not. Go on."

"Her daddy, Paddy McGee, was a great old guy. He hired me when no one else would. In fact, he and his wife took me in and fed me and gave me a bed to sleep on because they didn't like the idea of anybody sleeping in a car and doing without good food."

Billy thought for a moment about the day he'd met Paddy, the day the big, mostly gentle Irishman had taken him in. It wasn't a time in his life he was proud of, and he didn't want Arlene to know exactly how it had been.

Arlene wondered what Billy meant by "doing without good food," but the closed look on his face told her not to ask.

"Sherril, of course, was their daughter," he continued, taking her hand and holding it again. "Paddy and his wife were killed in a traffic accident six years after I met them." She heard the grief in his voice and knew he'd loved them. "A year later, when I was twenty-seven and Sherril was eighteen, I married her, so I guess you could call me something of a cradle robber. Only at the time, it was right. For both of us."

His eyes, and hers, went to the screen, where the young character Sherril played was framed in a close-up shot—flawless skin glowing, large eyes flashing with passion, red mouth pouting.

"She's very beautiful," said Arlene, "and she still looks eighteen."

Billy smiled. "She's very much like you," he said, startling her.

"Hardly!" She laughed as she looked from Billy's blue eyes back to the screen. If there was a resemblance, it was superficial; golden-brown hair, wide gray eyes, heart-shaped face. But Sherril was truly beautiful. Arlene was just . . . ordinary.

"Oh, yes. And when she really was eighteen, she was even more like you. Like you had been at that age." He let her hand go and turned her face toward him. "I was drawn to her . . . well, sexually, partly for that reason."

"Billy—" A nerve jumped in her lower abdomen and she shook her head, making his hand fall to the couch between them. The backs of his fingers rested against her upper leg. She flinched away from even that touch. "Don't do this. Don't say things . . . like that. There's no future in it, no point."

"You didn't let me finish," he murmured, and she nodded at him to go on.

"I may have been attracted to her initially because, as she grew up, she reminded me of you. But I stayed with her after we lost her parents—and married her—because I fell in love with her for herself." He sighed and looked back at the television, watching Sherril's character, Martina, walking away, disappearing offscreen.

"I'm sorry."

He lifted his brows. "What for?"

"Well, obviously you're not together any longer, and you love her very much. You're divorced?"

"Yes, but don't be sorry over that. Sure, I love her in lots of ways, but I'm no longer in love with her, nor she with me. We needed each other . . . for a time. And when that time was over, we were content to separate, live our lives the way each of us needs to. And remain the best of friends." His smile was sweet and warm and tender. "And she gave me Holly."

Arlene's eyes swung to the child slumped sideways in the big chair, her head on the armrest. She frowned. "Oh, look, she's fallen asleep!"

"Leave her." Billy's hand on her shoulder prevented her from getting up to tend to the child. "She always falls asleep as soon as Sherril says 'Good night, baby' on the show. I'll take her home in a few minutes. Think I could have some more coffee? I'd like to watch the rest of the show."

She hesitated. Watch the rest of the show? He'd hardly watched any of it so far. They'd been talking instead. Entertaining Billy and Holly was one thing; Billy, alone, quite another. However, good manners overcame good sense. At least one part of her insisted it was good manners that prompted the words. "I . . . yes, of course. But bring her over here to the couch and I'll cover her with the afghan. She looks so uncomfortable." Maybe Holly would wake up if she were moved.

No such luck.

Arlene poured more coffee and curled up by the little girl's feet, forcing Billy to take the chair his daughter had vacated. Without speaking, the two adults watched until the credits rolled up the screen, then, standing and stretching, Billy walked over and switched off the television set.

Arlene thought he would pick up his daughter then, and go home. But instead, he came and sat on the floor in front of the couch, arms wrapped around his knees, leaning back close to her legs. "Tell me about your day care program, Arlie."

She shrugged. "There's not a lot to tell. I run a private preschool and kindergarten for children with disabilities and, with a lot of help from my staff, provide day care for children whose parents work outside the home."

"I've been told by everyone that you've worked miracles with special-needs kids, that your training in the field is excellent and your expertise second to none."

"That's not true. People, well, sometimes people tend to exaggerate a bit, especially if they have a child they've been concerned about and that child starts to make progress."

His skeptical look told her he thought she was being modest. Uncomfortable, she got to her feet and went to the other side of the room, shoving back the drapes to look out. Turning back, she saw that Billy had risen to take her place on the sofa. He patted Holly's leg absently, gently, through the blanket, looking at Arlene, his eyes still questioning.

"But you *are* highly trained—an expert in dealing with special-needs kids," he insisted.

"All right, yes, I've had some very good training and a fair amount of experience. I've been in this business for a long time."

Standing, he tucked the afghan closer around Holly's feet, then came to where Arlene stood. "And the term 'special-needs,' " he asked, the skin around his mouth and eyes suddenly taut, his gaze holding hers intently, "does that include the bright as well as the . . . slow learners?"

Reluctantly, she nodded again, beginning to see where this conversation was leading. She had to derail it fast. "My training included teaching gifted children. My personal experience, however, isn't in that field." She felt hot and cold and scared and elated all at once. She shook her head. She didn't *want* Billy to need her. Not for anything! And certainly not for teaching his genius daughter. "I don't have enough experience, not the right kind, for what you want."

"Arlie, please—"

"Don't ask. I can't do it."

He looked tense. "I am asking. I have to. She needs you. Even the teachers at the academy won't be enough."

"No, Billy." She moved away from him. "Besides, there is no more Oakmount Academy. It burned down several years ago, and there simply aren't enough families raising their children on the Island to warrant rebuilding it. If you insist on living here, Holly will have to go to school in the Village."

"Forget that!" His objection was sharp but low in deference to the sleeping child. He followed Arlene, trapping her between the armchair and a bookcase, not touching her, but almost overwhelming her with his presence, his size, his desperation. His eyes blazed darkly, the blue shot with shafts of pewter.

"I will not send my daughter to the Village for her education! Holly has never attended a public school. Do you think I want the same thing done to her as was done to me? And I wasn't a genius, Arlie, I was just a little bit smarter than the average kid. After the hothouse atmosphere of the academy, my high school years in the Village came pretty damned close to shutting down my mind for good. Hell, I'd still be nothing more than a dropout if it hadn't been for a couple of good men who recognized my potential and forced me to complete my education."

"But—"

"The Village is out," he said flatly. "I went there. I know what kind of program they have. In elementary school they figure if they can keep the kids in their seats they've got it aced. In high school being a jock is far more important than being a brain."

"That was a long time ago. Things have changed. Public education has improved vastly. There's a good program for the gifted now in Juan de Fuca School, to name one. Go and see Frances Macomber, the principal, look over the school, see what you think. I believe you'll be pleasantly surprised. And as for after school, since you're 'retired,' surely you'll be able to provide that extra mental stimulation Holly needs?"

He shook his head, puffed out a harsh breath, and took her shoulders, giving her a small shake. She felt the tension in his fingers and wanted to soothe him, tell him how well she understood the frustrations of raising a child who was different. But she couldn't speak, could only stare at him in troubled silence as he said, "No, dammit! I have no patience! I can't teach her. Believe me, I've tried. Arlie, I'm begging for your help!"

He was begging, but she was quaking with fear, fear of what closer association with Billy's daughter could mean to her: closer association with Billy. She had to avoid that at all costs. Standing this close to him, feeling his warmth, breathing in his scent, made it almost impossible to deny him what he asked. If she spent any more time with him, when he asked for something else—and she knew he would—would she be able to deny him that? It was too risky. She had to keep their contact to a bare minimum.

"I'm sorry." Her voice trembled. She slipped her shoulders from under his warm hands and tried to slide past him, but he continued to block her way.

"Go away!" she cried in sudden frustration. "Get out of Oakmount! You don't *need* to live here! You've made an impulsive decision, one you'll probably change in a couple of weeks. You can live anywhere. A cramped little cottage is no place to raise your child when you can so well afford something better. Take Holly back to Phoenix, to her good school and the tutor she's used to. Or at least send her back until you're ready to leave here and join her. That would be best for her." *And for me!*

"I'm not taking Holly back to Phoenix, nor am I sending her back!" he shouted, completely forgetting that the subject of discussion lay sleeping not ten feet away. "How do you know what I need and don't need? I'm staying, Arlie, and Holly's staying with me. And she's not going to any penny-ante Village school! If I have to, I'll rebuild the academy and staff it myself. But believe me, whatever it takes, I mean to see that my daughter gets the best education possible, the one she deserves. And that she gets it right here on Oakmount Island."

"Goody, goody, goody," said a small, dry voice, and both adults whirled to see Holly sitting up rubbing one eye with her knuckles. With her other hand she pushed her hair back from her face. "But not only do I deserve a good education, Daddy, I deserve a good night's sleep as well, and I can't get it with you bellowing like that."

Billy subsided at once with a grin. He ran a hand through his hair. "Sorry," he said, "I guess I lost my head."

Holly giggled. "I like that expression. It conjures up such a wonderful picture."

"I'll bet it does," Billy said, scooping up his daughter and draping her upside down over his shoulder so her long hair fell in a smooth curtain, exposing her nape.

Arlene nearly cried out with the pain that sliced through her. Holly had the same strawberry birthmark that Billy had.

And Marcy.

The map of Montana.

Billy flipped Holly upright, then he reached out to touch Arlene's temple and froze. "What's wrong?" he asked quickly, his gaze intent.

"Nothing," she said. "Good night."

" 'Night, Arlie." Holly leaned forward in her father's arms and kissed Arlene on the cheek.

" 'Night," she said, her throat suddenly so thick she could scarcely force the word out.

Billy completed his arrested motion and stroked her cheek in the old way. "Sleep tight," he said softly with a smile that hurt her way down deep, where she lived.

As she closed the door, she wondered if she would sleep at all. Why hadn't she realized it before? Why hadn't it struck her?

That little girl was her daughter's sister.

And the two of them could never, ever meet.

SIX

"She's sure set that school on its ear!"

"Who has?" Arlene entered the big kitchen, which had, over the years, become the unofficial staff room of her school, and sat down at the table, reaching for the coffeepot.

"Billy Culver's little girl," said June Maybee, a long-time friend of Arlene's and one of the day care workers. Arlene carefully set the pot down, her cup only three-quarters full. So Billy had done the only thing possible if he intended to stay and keep his daughter with him; he'd placed Holly in a local school. Her stomach clenched. He was staying. She didn't know if she could stand it. She didn't know what she was going to do.

"Gail says the principal asked her to set up some math programs for Holly," June went on, slicing a loaf of banana bread. "The kid went through the work sheets in an hour and a half and looked around for more. They were supposed to keep her busy for a couple of weeks." June's sister, Gail, Arlene knew, taught sixth grade at Juan de Fuca School.

"I heard that she tests out at over one-sixty-five," said Maggie Leighton. "And that Frankie said she didn't want any part of her. But Billy turned on the charm and she found herself enrolling the kid in spite of her better judgment. An eight-year-old with an IQ that high needs a slick father, I guess, to clear a path for her. I don't think a lot of principals would be eager to take on a child with those kinds of needs."

"High IQ doesn't have to be a problem," said Arlene. Of course, in the case of her little school and day care, it was. She wasn't set up for a child with Holly's special needs. The public school, however, damned well was, and if it wasn't, it should be.

"All the staff at Juan de Fuca have to do is make a small amount of extra effort to find things to keep Holly interested. If they start focusing on her and considering her a 'problem' student, they're going to end up with exactly the kind of problem they're afraid of having." She took a slice of banana bread from the plate June had set on the table and bit into it.

"Like father like daughter?" said June, who knew as well as Arlene the legends of Billy Culver—and viewed them with a certain amount of awe.

"Probably not, so don't get excited." Arlene had to swallow before she could laugh. "For one thing, I doubt that Holly is going to build a moonshine still on the roof of the gym the way her father did."

Then, quickly, she changed the subject, trying not to think about Holly. Or Billy. But his blue eyes pleading, his voice saying, "I'm asking. I have to," haunted her, and she found herself coming back again and again to the thought that maybe Holly did need her. That maybe she could help. What if it were Marcy? What if her daughter, her darling, handicapped daughter, had been refused the education she needed, the help?

She finally decided if she did agree to tutor Holly, and it did mean closer contact with Billy, she could keep their relationship on an old-friend basis. After all, they'd been friends for much longer than they'd been lovers! In fact, they'd hardly been lovers at all, when it came right down to it. She knew the attraction she still felt for him was wrong, possibly even immoral, and since she was a good person, she would never succumb.

So, when the principal of Juan de Fuca School phoned her on Friday morning, her heart leapt. She couldn't contain her delight at having been asked officially for help. If it was official, how could she say no?

"Can you come to a staff meeting this afternoon, Arlene?" Frankie sounded distracted and disturbed. "I really need your help. I'm going to have a revolt on my hands if I don't get someone in here to give my people some guidelines for dealing with Holly Culver. The child is driving us right up the wall. Her mind knows no limits, and she's constantly demanding input. Input we don't have. So will you come and talk to us this afternoon? I've called a meeting for four-thirty. And see if you can look up some literature on teaching the gifted for me, will you? I need all the help I can get."

Arlene gave a resigned sigh. So, it would seem, did Holly. Not once had Frankie suggested that maybe the child was as unhappy as the staff. "Fine, then. I'll be there." She'd wanted to get some paperwork out of the way that afternoon and evening so she could get away early Saturday morning for her weekend with Marcy. Still, how could she abandon a little girl who clearly needed a champion?

Arlene came to a halt inside the door of the meeting room, clutching her briefcase under one arm and staring at the assembled teachers—and one parent, who turned to look at her. *Billy*. She should have expected it. Yet she hadn't.

Her pulse rate skyrocketed and her face flushed. She hoped it might be put down to the fact that she was ten minutes late and had been rushing. To her relief, the principal noticed her arrival and spoke up, jerking her gaze from Billy's.

"Arlene, come on in. Coffee?" Frankie bustled around, filling cups, chatting, trying, Arlene thought, to keep the meeting at an informal level. "Here, sit down," she said, pulling out a chair beside Billy's at one end of the long, oval table. "We'll get started as soon as everyone's here. I'm so glad you could come." The principal, a large, stout woman in a green dress, left them to help one of her teachers wrestle a folding blackboard into position near the table.

"I'm glad you could come too," said Billy. "Looks like I've got a budding problem here." His concerned gaze met hers. There were a pair of vertical lines between his black brows. She wanted to smooth them away with the tip of a finger. She wanted to put her arms around him and hug him tightly. She wanted . . . she wanted things that weren't possible and forced herself to look upon him as nothing more than the parent of a student, one who needed all the help she could give.

"Don't worry," she said quietly with a reassuring smile. "We'll sort it out. They only need to understand the situation."

"I spent over an hour yesterday trying to make the principal understand and got nowhere."

Arlene felt herself begin to relax slightly, felt her heart rate slide down the scale toward normal, and hoped her flush was fading. She reminded herself that she could deal with Billy as a friend. She would refuse to think of the other emotions he continued to arouse in her. They could be controlled. And look at him. He wasn't doing a thing to suggest he wanted her to be more than a champion for his child.

"I'm glad you're on our side," he said, suddenly wrapping his warm hand around her wrist and taking her hand down under the table to lay it on his thigh. So much for all the comforting thoughts she'd been deluding herself with. She met the intensity of his gaze. Her heart began a crazy cadence again as she read in his eyes questions she dared not answer.

"I'm on Holly's side," she said, and heard the breathless note in her voice. He'd heard it too. His eyes darkened and a soft smile played on his mouth.

"You've always been on my side," he said with utmost confidence. "That's why I asked Mrs. Macomber to invite you to this meeting."

Frankie broke in on their private conversation before Arlene could reply. "We're all here," she said. "Let's get to it."

As two more teachers took seats around the table, she turned on a tape recorder. "Now that we're all assembled, I'll start by outlining some of the difficulties we've run into in the past week, trying to assimilate Holly Culver, a very bright child, into our little school with its very average population of students and teachers."

When Frankie had completed her opening remarks, she turned the meeting over to Arlene, who spent an hour explaining what Holly's needs were, and how the staff could help her fulfill them, offering her own resources where they were needed. The only sour note was when Holly's teacher, John Elkworth, flatly refused to have her in his room another day, and stormed out of the meeting, saying that he was running a third-grade class, not an experimental lab.

"You've been a wonderful help," Frankie said when Arlene finally sat down. "Thank you."

"Don't thank me, or if you must, do it by ensuring that Holly is accepted in this school by students and teachers alike." Once more, she looked slowly around the table and met each pair of eyes. Most reflected shame and shock at what one of their members had said and done. "She has as much need and right as any other child to be with other kids on a regular basis. It's the only way she'll continue to develop basic social skills and to grow to psychological maturity along with her peers.

"Thank you all for listening. Frankie will pass along any concerns you may have as different problems arise."

"Come and have dinner with me. And Holly," Billy added as Arlene whirled from the door of her car in response to his touch on her elbow. "I have to walk over to the library and pick her up. She's been with Miss Quail."

"Billy . . ." Her eyes were caught and held for a moment before she tore them away from the smoldering heat in his. "No. Thank you, but no."

"It's only to say thanks for what you did in there," he said.

She let out an impatient puff of breath. "Like I told Frankie, I don't want thanks. I'm simply doing what's right for a student in this district."

"Bull—" he started to say, but broke off as Holly came bounding up to them.

"Daddy! Hi, Arlie. I saw you guys over here and Miss Quail said I could cross the street by myself if I waited for the light. She doesn't know I always wait for the light. Well, nearly always. I have a million things to tell you about school. Look . . ." Holly pulled a neatly folded paper from her jeans pocket. "I got all my spelling right," she said, but then looked glum. "Only I didn't get a gold star. Julie did, but Mr. Elkworth said I'd get my spelling right regardless of what words he gave me, so a gold star wouldn't be any encouragement."

Arlene and Billy exchanged a quick look, and Billy said, "One of the things that was decided in that meeting, Holly, is that Mr. Elkworth won't be your teacher anymore."

"He won't?" Holly brightened, then looked worried again. "But who will I get, Daddy? None of them really like me. I make too much work for them."

Arlene couldn't stand it. She wondered if any teacher had ever made her own daughter feel that way, and prayed that it wasn't so. When it came to special needs, and a lot of work, Marcy's needs were so much greater than Holly's that there couldn't even be a comparison. On an impulse she knew she would live to regret, but which she couldn't not act on, she bent to hug the little girl and say, "Tell you what. When you come to my house on Monday after school for our first session together, I'll give you a gold star. I have lots of them."

"Our first . . . session?" Hope and joy dawned on Holly's face. "Oh, Arlie! You're going to do it? Be my tutor? Is she, Daddy? Really?"

"First I've heard of it," Billy said.

To Arlene's shock, his blue eyes sheened over. Her own would have flooded if she'd had to go on looking at him, seeing the intensity of his gratitude, the depth of his relief, the— She didn't know what else she thought she read in his eyes, but it moved her profoundly. And filled her with fear.

Only she knew she had to do this thing, regardless of the consequences.

Quickly, she turned back to Billy's daughter. "I want to be your tutor, Holly."

Holly squealed and flung her arms around Arlene, hugging tightly. "Oh, thank you, thank you. Dad says you're one smart, smart lady and can teach me a whole lot. Now, can we have dinner? You're coming too, aren't you, Arlie? Daddy promised he'd ask you. Did he?"

Arlene allowed herself to be towed toward the inn's swaying wooden sign. Billy had promised Holly to ask her for dinner? She sighed silently, wishing she didn't feel so let down that he hadn't asked her because *he* wanted to be with her. It was irrational, unreasonable, and she was going to have to do something about her foolish tendency to slip back into patterns of the past.

"Evening, Miss Lambert." Eddie Markham wiped his hands on his crisp white apron and pulled out a chair for Arlene. "Well, Billy," he said, seating the little girl next, "I see you brought reinforcements tonight. Though you didn't need to. Ellen called in sick today." He grinned slyly. "Could be she's all tuckered out. There were a couple of suits and ties in here last night for dinner. She hit it off just fine with one of them. Wouldn't be surprised if she took him home with her. Ya lost your chance there, boy." He cut another sly glance Arlene's way. "Though I don't suppose you mind a whole helluva lot?"

Billy gave him a level stare, ignoring the question. "Evening, Eddie. Have you met my daughter, Holly? Holly, this is Mr. Markham. He owns the inn and cooks those burgers you like so much."

Eddie gave a small shrug and solemnly shook hands with the child. "How do, little lady? Like my hamburgers, do you? Well, you sit tight and I'll send the waitress over to you right away."

Dinner was a more relaxed meal than Arlene had anticipated, with Holly's sprightly chatter keeping the conversation lively. She demanded stories about Billy's childhood, about her grandmother, about

Arlene and Billy, as children. Arlene found herself laughing more than she had in years, sharing jokes, reminiscences, even lighthearted arguments with Billy over certain points of fact on which they differed. But it was the laughter she loved, and she knew she'd cherish the memory of this meal with Billy and his daughter for the rest of her life.

"Know what?" Billy said, drawing one finger from her wrist to the tip of her index finger. "I'm having fun."

"Yes," she said. He'd just put her thoughts into words. She smiled and turned her hand so that their fingers meshed. "Me too, Billy. Thank you for asking me to join you."

His hand squeezed hers tightly. "Thank you for coming." He chewed on his lower lip for a moment, looking at her, those myriad questions in his eyes once more. "I can't remember the last time I felt like this. Why don't the three of us do something together for the weekend?"

Arlene jerked her hand back as temptation jolted through her.

"I have plans for the weekend," she said, and stood. "I need to get home now. Have a nice weekend, you two."

"Wait," said Holly. "We're coming too."

As they walked back out to their cars, Arlene had to laugh at Holly's delight in the silver spangles of frost on every bush and tuft of grass, and the little clouds her breath made. She was enthralled by the patterns of frost on the windshields.

"That looks like the wallpaper in my bedroom," she said while Billy held her up so she could scrape the windshield of Arlene's car. "Daddy and I repapered it yesterday, Arlene. Come and see it, okay?"

"Yeah," said Billy, setting his daughter down. His

eyes met Arlene's for a potent second. "Come and see it. I'll even make you a better cup of coffee than old Eddie manages."

"Please?" Holly looked up, her eyes pleading. "And then we can discuss what my last tutor and I were working on."

"I have a lot to do," she said, but Billy touched her cheek in that way he had, and she swung her gaze to meet his again.

"Only one coffee," he said quietly, and in his eyes she saw he meant it. He wasn't going to push her. He wasn't going to ask anything of her she wasn't prepared to give. But he didn't yet want the evening to end.

And neither, she had to admit, did she.

She, like Billy, was reluctant to let go of the pleasure they'd been sharing. But unlike Billy, she also knew that it was pleasure they weren't entitled to.

Still, as she had throughout the week, she asked herself again, was it so wrong to enjoy friendship? Didn't everyone need it? And as long as it remained strictly platonic—"only one coffee"—what was the harm?

"Thanks, I'd like that," she said, and tried to ignore the steady, deep throbbing in her soul, and the ever-present chant. *Billy . . . Billy . . . Billy . . .*

"You said the other night that a couple of 'good men' made you complete your education." Arlene was sitting with her feet on the hearth, watching the crackling flames of the fire Billy had lit. The brandy in her coffee was warm inside her. It buzzed pleasantly in her head. The warmth enfolded her, as did the quiet. For twenty minutes she and Billy had been sitting silently, listening to the snapping of burning wood and the soft sounds coming from the stereo in the corner. Holly was asleep in her bedroom with the feather-patterned wallpaper.

As she spoke, Arlene turned her head and looked at Billy. He sat, as she did, in an overstuffed chair pulled up to the fire. "One, I gathered, was Paddy McGee. Who was the other?"

"Glenn Klemchuck. You may have heard Holly speak of her uncle Glenn. He's my lawyer, my good friend and sometimes partner, in that he invests in every venture of mine."

"You have a lot of ventures, don't you?" Arlene asked. "You're one of the main backers of *The Great Divide.*" She sat up just long enough to reach for her cup, then leaned back against the pillowy chair. Billy had replaced all the old furniture with soft, comfortable modern stuff. She liked it and wished she could take this chair home with her. It was no wonder she'd stayed longer than she'd planned. She was too comfortable to move. And too content. It was good, sitting like this, talking to Billy. Seventeen years was a long, long time to go without a best friend.

He shrugged. "The show more than pays its own way, but yeah, maybe I helped get it started."

She had to smile at his self-effacement. It was completely out of character. Or would have been. Billy, she already knew, had changed, matured, and she liked the man he'd become very, very much. As much as the girl she had been had liked the boy. She wished . . . There was no point in futile wishes, she decided, and squelched that one quickly. "Tell me about what you do."

"I already did," he said with an irrepressible grin that brought back to mind the old Billy. "I'm retired. Being retired is what I do."

She laughed at him, at this vital, dynamic man with his black hair, his striking blue eyes, his zest for life. "Why don't I believe you?" she asked.

He joined in her laughter. The sounds blended nicely, warmly, creating a cocoon of happiness around them. "Because you know me so well?"

She sighed softly. "I used to, Billy."

He stroked the back of her wrist with one finger. "Do you want to again?"

She didn't dare answer that. Not even to herself. In order to break free of his touch, she lifted her cup and sipped again, then leaned forward and set it on the hearth, empty. "Tell me how you got started in business."

He removed his hand from the arm of her chair and ran it into his hair. "I don't know where to begin. Most of what happened to me sort of, well, just happened. It was luck, every bit of it, and meeting the right people at the right time, learning from them and applying that knowledge."

"What people? Paddy? Glenn?"

"Yeah, but not Glenn at first. First it was Paddy McGee." He half stood and hitched his chair around to face her at right angles, then propped his feet on the hearth only inches from hers. "Paddy, my savior. He was the making of the man I became. He looked at the useless boy and saw something inside, though God knows what."

He was silent until she asked, "Then what?"

"Then he went mining for it, quarried it out. I fought and kicked and screamed and threatened to leave because his digging into my soul hurt like hell. All day I worked for him. Slaved! And every evening we talked, even when I didn't want to. Even when I told him to mind his own business and forget about me, he got me talking and kept me talking.

"But somehow, even when I swore I hated him, I never got around to leaving. Paddy was the first person who'd treated me like a human being for quite a while, and I guess I needed that. He and Mrs. McGee were real good to me."

"That night we watched *The Great Divide* together, you said Paddy and his wife fed you when you were . . . 'doing without good food.' Why weren't you eating right?"

"Money, honey. Or the lack thereof. I'd gone from one dead-end job to another, and the spells between them were getting longer and longer. I couldn't see it then, but it was because I had a chip on my shoulder as big as a redwood. A real attitude problem. I met Paddy when he flattened me with a right hook to the jaw. He thought I was trying to break into the back room of his restaurant. I wasn't. I was looking for a box to help me get into the dumpster to find something to eat. He grabbed me by the scruff of the neck, spun me around, and smacked me into next week."

"Billy!" The horror in her eyes cut into him, making him sorry he'd told her. "You were so hungry you had to do that? Why didn't you call—" She broke off, biting her lip, and shook her head. "No. I guess you couldn't call, could you?"

She lowered her eyes, thinking about one reason her father had likely had for sending Billy away the day they buried his mother. Resolutely, she pushed that thought out of her mind. She would think of it tomorrow. Yeah. She and Scarlett.

"It was a long time ago, sweetheart," Billy said comfortingly, stroking her instep with his toes. "And it's all over now. Don't agonize over it. I don't. And maybe it was good for me, taught me a bit of tolerance for the truly unfortunate in the world."

She pulled her feet away, tucking them under her in her chair. "Why'd you do that?" he said, looking injured. "I was just touching your foot."

"I . . . I don't know." On the face of it, her reaction had been stupid. He *had* just been touching her foot. He'd meant nothing sexual by it, nothing she should be concerned about. It had simply been a friendly gesture, one friend to another. A touch of comfort, because she was unhappy, thinking about his unhappy past. He wasn't responsible for the thrill that had run through her body at his touch and centered low in her belly, gathering force, especially with his next words.

"I'm a toucher, Arlie. I always have been. You know that."

"I know. I . . . remember." But she didn't put her feet back where he could reach them. What she had to do was forget.

"Paddy and Mrs. McGee were great," he said after looking at her thoughtfully for a moment. "They took me in, fed me, gave me a bed. They even gave me a job because I couldn't get one anywhere else and because that was their way. I washed dishes for them." He pulled a face. "And bused tables, did a little kitchen prep, and cleaned a lot of floors. I hated every minute of it, but it was work, and they paid me and kept me from going hungry, so I did it."

"They didn't need mechanics in Phoenix?"

He laughed quietly, shaking his head in rueful memory. "I was no mechanic, Arlie. Old Mortimer hired me out of the goodness of his heart and let me do lube jobs and tire changes. I didn't realize that at the time, of course. I thought I was a hotshot grease monkey. It took only a couple of days in a real shop to teach me that I knew less than nothing and didn't have the aptitude to learn or the patience to try. If I'd been any good, I could have kept my car on the road instead of letting it break down irreparably a few days after I left here.

"So there I was, sleeping in that old Ford in an alley, getting more and more scared, more and more hungry, and more and more homesick, even though I didn't have a home to be sick over. Then Paddy turned up, and like I said, he gave me a home. As grateful as I was, after four or five months in his restaurant, we both knew I wasn't cut out for that kind of life. He asked me what I wanted to do, but I didn't know."

He grinned at the memories swirling through his mind. "He had some weird and wonderful ideas, which is probably why a guy named Patrick McGee owned and operated a Chinese restaurant and did all the cooking himself. No one ever told him that Irishmen can't cook Chinese, so he did a great job. He figured that if doctors can decide on the specialty they want by interning in different hospital departments, maybe it would work for me. He lined up a series of jobs with friends of his—a guy in real estate, a woman who did landscaping, and next, a glazier. I broke more glass than I ever installed, and that one lasted only about two weeks. And then I met Glenn Klemchuck." He grinned again and blew out a long breath.

"He's a lawyer, like I said. He put me to work researching title deeds, finding missing heirs, and digging out properties about to be sold for back taxes and contacting the people who might have wanted to buy them. It was the most fascinating work I'd ever done, and before I knew it, my three-month 'internship' was up, and I didn't want to leave.

"Between them, Glenn and Paddy made me leave, though. They sent me to school. They wouldn't let me work my way through, so I studied hard and learned fast in order to get out and get a job so I could pay them back. All this time I lived with Paddy and Mrs. McGee and Sherril over the Chinese restaurant. I got my MBA in record time and went to work for Fordham Industries.

"They're a development company. I worked for them for a couple of years, then got a lucky break.

I managed to buy an apartment building Glenn knew about that was on the skids and up for a tax sale.

"I put everything into that building I could get my hands on, and after the renovations were finished and the place was rented out again, I was able to pay Paddy and Glenn back for my education. I made enough profit on the first building to buy my next tax-sale property, and then I was on my own. And from there on, it sort of came together. Like I said, I was lucky."

"And smart," she said, smiling at him. "Don't you think smart had anything to do with it?"

He shrugged. "Maybe a little." He slid down in his chair, linked his hands behind his head, and stared into the fire again. "An irony just struck me. If I'd known the cottage was mine right from the beginning, and lived here, I would have lost it to somebody like me, somebody who could come up with the money for the taxes. With what I was earning, I couldn't have paid them."

"My grandmother did," she said, and knew even as she said it that Letitia would never have done so if Billy had been living there.

"Yeah. So I'd never get a tax notice and know it was mine." He fixed her with a hard look for a moment. "For the same reason you paid them, right?"

She sighed. "Yes."

"And you wonder why I was pissed off?"

She shook her head. "No. I don't wonder. I simply didn't know what else to do," she said tautly, and got to her feet. "I better be going, Billy. Thanks for the coffee." She smiled faintly. "And the conversation."

He stood and stepped close to her. Too close. "Thanks for the company, Arlie. It gets lonely here in the evenings after Holly's gone to bed."

"Yes." She swallowed, stepped back from him, and grabbed her coat. Did he think he had the corner on loneliness? Taking her coat from her, he helped her on with it, then turned her, buttoning it for her.

She tried to brush his hands away. "I can do that," she protested.

"So can I." Then, with his fists clenched around her lapels, he pulled her against him and pressed a hard, determined kiss on her lips, parting them with his tongue, barely touching the inner sides, making them tingle and burn, creating a slow volcano of heat inside her. She jumped back, staring at him.

"Good night, sweet Arlie. Can we do this again?"

He laughed softly at the alarm that leapt into her gray eyes. "This?" she said.

"Dinner. Coffee. Conversation."

"I . . . oh. Yes. I suppose so."

His grin was pure Billy, all raffish and wicked. "And this," he said, sliding his arms around her, his lips hovering a centimeter from hers. They touched hers briefly.

"No . . ." she breathed. "No. Not . . . that."

"Sorry," he murmured. "Too late." And he kissed her again, longer, but with such tenderness she felt herself melting against him, curling into his warmth, her arms sliding around his middle. This time he was the one to step back.

With an arm around her shoulders he walked her out onto the porch and stood while she got in her car.

"I'll be watching for your bedroom light to come on," he said, and she quickly slammed her door.

Dammit, she thought when she finally slid into bed, not to sleep but to toss and turn and twist. It was all Billy's fault she couldn't get the rest she needed. He'd come back into her life as big and as brash as ever, turning her inside out and messing up her libido, which, prior to his return, had settled fairly nicely into a quiet little hum, very seldom disturbed. A couple of weeks ago she might have thought that was sad, and wondered why she put up with such a drab, sterile life. Now, however, she realized she hadn't known when she was well off. The feelings she'd been experiencing since her past had returned to haunt her were almost impossible to withstand—especially when she had no possible outlet for them.

And what about Billy? Judging by what Eddie had suggested, he wasn't having any difficulty finding an outlet for his libido. Not that that was news, of course. But Ellen? Arlene pulled a face and rolled over again. Why not Ellen? It wouldn't, she was certain, be the first time Billy had dated the woman who had been known as a good backseat romp when they were teenagers.

She sighed, tugged her pillow into a better position, and closed her eyes, glad with all her might that one of the "suits and ties" Eddie had mentioned had come along to take up Ellen's interest. It wasn't that she wanted Billy for herself, of course. It couldn't be that, because she knew she couldn't have him, ever.

That was one of those basic facts of life she'd had to accept over the years. It was non-negotiable. But that didn't mean she had to think Ellen would be good for Billy.

And why wouldn't she? It was as if Billy's voice were speaking inside her mind. *You don't want me. You've made that clear enough, so why shouldn't I get my release where I can, with anyone I can?*

"You can, for all I care," she said aloud, flopping onto her back and staring up at the dark ceiling. "But not with her."

Why not her? I have before, Arlie, and believe me, it was more rewarding than having a scared little virgin—who cried, for heaven's sake! Why do you think I left?

Why do you think I never came back? You weren't worth coming back to.

She sighed loudly. And that was when the phone rang.

"I called to say good-night and ask if you remembered to lock your door."

"Billy! Of course I locked my door. Good night."

"Were you asleep?"

"Just about."

"Funny, you don't sound sleepy. You sound as wide awake as I am."

"I don't know how wide awake you are, so I can't comment. But I do have to get up early, so why don't you hang up the phone and let me get some sleep?"

"You hang up first."

She had to smile. "You called me. You hang up."

He laughed. "You remember those dumb conversations we used to have too."

"What dumb conversations?" she said with the lofty insouciance of a fourteen-year-old. "I've forgotten."

"Liar. Arlie, what would you say if I told you I had no intention of staying in Oakmount until after I saw you again?"

"I'd say you should pack up and leave, Billy."

"What about my property here on the Island? Do you want it?"

She was silent for several moments. "I can't afford it, Billy. But maybe one of the other owners would take it."

"Nope. If I sell my holdings on the Island, I'll sell to you or to no one."

She had to laugh. *"Holdings?* A two-bedroom cottage and half an acre of land are hardly holdings, Billy."

"Sorry. A term I'm accustomed to using. What if I don't sell you my cottage but give it to you?"

"Why would you want to do that?"

"Oh, I don't know. Wedding present, maybe?"

"I have no intention of getting married, and even if I did, I don't think it would be . . . appropriate."

"No? Maybe not." He conceded so quickly, she knew he'd never meant it in the first place. He was toying with her. Teasing. She wished she knew why. Oh, hell, she knew why. Because he was Billy Culver!

There was nothing for her to say except "Good night, Billy."

His chuckle was soft and full of triumph. " 'Night, Arlie. Sleep tight."

He hung up first.

Arlene slept with a smile on her face and a thousand questions in her heart which, upon wakening, she knew would never be answered.

They should never have even been asked.

SEVEN

"What do you think about the rumors, Arlene?" It was Monday morning, and Arlene was just making the coffee when June Maybee arrived at six-thirty, fifteen minutes before the first of the day care kids.

Sleepily, she looked at her friend. "What rumors are those?"

"About the new development. Hey, come on. Wake up. Where have you been all weekend?"

"In Seattle with Marcy. Why? And what's new about those rumors? They've been going on ever since the mill went down to one shift. Something fantastic's going to come along and save Oakmount. I'll believe it when I see it."

"God, I'm surprised the entire population of Oakmount Island didn't start phoning you the minute you crossed the bridge last night," said June. "All the Islanders are up in arms. Seems the owner of that property your family dumped after your grandpa got sick is going to put in a boat-building operation right out here on your clean, exclusive shores and hire a bunch of local people to work in it."

Arlene laughed. "Don't be silly. We're not zoned for that kind of development on Oakmount Island."

"Seems you are, and that the new owner doesn't care about all that exclusivity. What with permitting the marina, to say nothing of this school, the Island lost its strictly residential zoning a few years back."

June's attitude was one of subtle, perhaps even unintentional triumph, and not for the first time, Arlene was painfully aware that she would never be fully accepted by the townspeople as one of them. Not even by June, her closest friend. No matter that she worked for a living as they did, that she was admired and even respected for her work with children who would otherwise have to go into the city for their education, she would always, on one level, be one of the rich, resented Islanders.

The coffee maker gurgled and the aroma filled the air. Arlene drew in an appreciative breath of it. "You shouldn't listen to rumors," she said quietly. "You may not be aware of it, but there's a covenant that every Islander signed upon purchasing land here. It regulates whom he can sell to, and none of us have been asked to approve a new owner, so what you've heard is impossible."

June frowned. "I don't think so, and part of it's more than a rumor, Arlene. Look at this." She held up the Saturday edition of the local paper, which Arlene had dumped unread on the table Sunday night. "A public meeting wouldn't be held to discuss a rumor, would it?"

" 'S&H Development invites you to an informational meeting regarding a new and exciting venture planned for the town of Oakmount . . .' " Arlene sat down hard on a chair. So it was more than a rumor that something was coming down. "But it doesn't say anything about the Island."

"I know, but people are saying that they've seen men taking surveys over here, right on the big chunk of land that used to belong to your family. There seems to have been a lot of stuff going on very quietly over the past couple of months. I think the rumors are right—whatever's happening is going to happen on the Island."

"There certainly seems to be some kind of development planned, but it's not going to be out here. Maybe there's some wishful thinking on the part of a few Villagers who resent the locked gate that keeps us private." She knew it was human nature to be peeved by notions of exclusivity in others, and she understood it, sympathized with it. But facts were facts, and the Islanders had always had a gate to protect them from unwelcome visitors. Once, it had been manned by guards; now, every owner had both a key and a buzzer, the latter to let in outsiders.

June shrugged and looked momentarily uncomfortable. "Maybe, but I got that information on Saturday night at the inn, from Ellen Mortimer. She'd been dating a guy named Jacob Aaronson, one of the movers and shakers behind the plan. Ellen couldn't wait to let everyone know that she had some inside information."

Arlene stared at June. Ellen *had* been dating what Eddie Markham called a "suit and tie." She might be in the know. "What does it mean?" she asked, not expecting an answer.

The block of land her father had unloaded had come on the market again eight or nine years ago. She, along with the other Islanders, had been informed that it was up for sale. There was no way she could buy it, and she was quite certain the asking price was beyond any other individual Islander as well. Then, when nothing further had been said, when the Island Land Owners' Association hadn't been asked to approve the credentials of a potential purchaser, she'd forgotten about it, assumed that the vendor had withdrawn.

She frowned. But did the covenant prevent an

owner from developing his land? It would seem not. "Oh, brother," she said slowly, her eyes focusing on June's face again. "If all of this is true, there's bound to be a battle royal between Island and Village, starting right about now."

"You're not kidding! But what do you mean, starting now? It's been going on all weekend—ever since this notice came out."

That was when the phone started ringing.

For the next couple of hours, Arlene talked to friends and neighbors, all of whom thought for several reasons that she would be in the know, and all of whom implied that since she was a Lambert, it was somehow her fault.

"That boat yard is going to be adjacent to my property!" wept elderly Janine Hamilton, which wasn't surprising; Janine cried whenever an occasion arose. "And yours too. It will separate us, Arlene, divide the Island! You have to do something."

"But what?"

"I don't know! You're the Lambert. Your forefathers owned the Island originally, laid out the rules for its settlement, rules that are being threatened. Think about it. Our peace disturbed by comings and goings of boats at all hours of the day and night. People coming over the bridge every day to work here. Riffraff, Arlene. Itinerants. None of us will be safe. Our security is at an end. You must find a way to stop it. What are we going to do?"

"Mrs. Hamilton, I'm sorry. I don't know anything more than you do. But I understand there is a public meeting in the Village hall tonight at seven-thirty. I plan to be there. I suggest you arrange to attend as well. Shall I pick you up?"

Mrs. Hamilton agreed and Arlene hung up, frowning, and turned on her answering machine so she could concentrate on her students. But her concentration was poor. She was concerned and disturbed by all the elitist talk she'd heard. She assured herself that they didn't mean to be snobbish and unkind. Most of the Islanders were old. They were simply accustomed to the status quo and were fearful of change.

The meeting that evening did nothing to allay the fears of the Islanders or to ease Arlene's misgivings about their attitude. Frequent furors arose to protest each new announcement made by Jacob Aaronson, the agent for S&H Development.

"Silence! Silence!" The mayor banged her gavel on the desk before her. "I will have order here!" Order was not easily restored as people stared at each other with glazed, disbelieving eyes, asking questions that went unheard, unanswered. Rental units? Tract housing? On Oakmount Island?

As the din continued, Billy crowded into the row of chairs where Arlene sat, asked two people to move down a bit, and slid onto the chair next to her. His laughing gaze caught hers, and his broad shoulder pressed against her as he slouched in his chair. He lifted his brows, then shook his head, saying, "Tsk, tsk, what an uproar!"

Arlene pursed her lips and broke the hold of his gaze, determined not to share his amusement, wishing he had sat anywhere but right beside her. When he was this close, it was too hard to remember why she had to keep their relationship the same as it had been when she was six years old. When he was this close, she didn't feel like a six-year-old.

"And now," Jacob Aaronson said finally, closing his portfolio on the easel at the front of the room, "I'm open for questions from the floor."

Billy chuckled. "What does he think he's been getting all along?"

"A hard time," Arlene murmured before she

could bite back the words. Against her arm she felt Billy's silent laugh and shifted away again.

Arlene was glad when the mayor declared the meeting over. She stood to stretch her cramped muscles. She'd sat too rigid, trying not to let Billy lean on her.

"Well, now," he said, taking her hand and tucking it under his arm as she walked with Mrs. Hamilton to the car. She couldn't pull away without making a scene. "Interesting state of affairs, isn't it, ladies?" He had a slight frown on his face, and questions in his eyes. More of that devilish laughter too. "What do you think of it, Arlie?"

She tugged her hand free and unlocked the car, opening the passenger door for the elderly lady, seeing her seated comfortably before closing the door and replying to Billy's question. "I don't know," she said honestly. "I think it could be good for the Village, and Lord knows we need jobs here for the young people." She opened her car door and slid onto the seat. "One thing worries me, though—what Aaronson said about highly trained workers. How many people in Oakmount are highly trained in any aspect of boat building or repair?"

Billy was completely taken aback. Arlene *liked* the idea of the development? Maybe she was just kidding. He scowled. If she wasn't, if she did think it was a good thing, she was the only Islander who did. He was glad of that. What the hell would be the point in getting them riled up if they wouldn't cooperate? He tried not to feel too good about Arlene's actually liking his plan. Of course, she didn't know it was his. Would she change her mind if she did?

He forced down his reaction and said coolly, "That's a good point. You think maybe there won't be as many jobs for locals as that guy Aaronson is making out?"

"I think it needs to be looked into."

"I guess." He shrugged nonchalantly. "Can you give me a ride home? I walked over." Reaching behind her, Arlene unlocked a back door and Billy got in, rubbing his cold hands together. Arlene closed her door, started the engine, and turned up the heater.

"You brought up an important issue, Mrs. Hamilton," Billy said as they headed across the bridge, "when you asked about ecological damage." He'd expected the question, but not from the likes of her.

"I certainly did, young man. I read the papers and watch television. I know what's a hot issue nowadays. If anything will get a few TV stations and politicians on our side, that's what it will be. And I don't believe for one minute what that slick agent said about sealed systems, sewage treatment, and toxic waste controls. Workers are sloppy, given half a chance. If nobody's looking, a man's as likely as not to dump his paint thinner behind a rock rather than take it to where it can be disposed of safely."

"You may be right, Mrs. Hamilton. It will certainly bear watching once the yard is in production."

"Young man, you don't think for a minute, do you, that this boat yard will ever be built?" she asked, aghast.

"I . . . well, it seemed from what we heard tonight, Mrs. Hamilton, that it's going to happen," Billy said mildly. "The meeting wasn't a public hearing at which the company was required to show cause for requesting a zone change or anything like that. Since no change was required, the council had no legitimate reason to refuse the application. Tonight's meeting was just what the paper said, wasn't

it? An informational meeting so we could all learn
what the company has in mind."

"Maybe that's what you think, but I think we are
going to band together, we Islanders, and fight, and
win."

"We, as Islanders, may well band together, Mrs.
Hamilton," he said, deliberately including himself,
holding back a laugh when he saw her shoulders
stiffen in indignation. "And we may fight. But I
assure you, we won't win."

"How can you possibly know that? And why
would someone like you care, Billy Culver? You
aren't one of us in spite of the judge's having left
your mother that cottage. How dare you call yourself an Islander?"

She began to weep. "They should have sent you
away when you killed my boy Curtis all those years
ago! You were a bad one then, and I don't suppose
you've changed. Of course you'll side with the Villagers on this issue! You're like them. They're
greedy, grasping looters, all, wanting to take what
we have and ruin it, *ruin it*, I tell you, simply
because they're jealous! Is that why you came back,
Billy Culver? To get a job in that boat yard? Well,
you may as well leave! There won't be a boat yard.
We'll fight. We'll fight you, and those like you, right
to the end. There will be no rental units built on
Oakmount Island!"

The old dame might as well have said leper col-
ony. Billy's temper flared out of control. "And that's
what you're most concerned with, isn't it, you old
bat? You don't care about the ecology, except when
it seems expedient! You'd use those fears only to
throw a monkey wrench into things, wouldn't you?
Use popular, motherhood issues in order to suck in
politicians, television, and other media, purely for
your own selfish ends!

"And no, for your information, I did not come

back to get a job in the boat yard! How could I? It wasn't even announced until tonight. And I'll tell you one more thing. I might well take what you have, but not because I'm jealous, Mrs. Hamilton, because I'm rich! Filthy rich! I can buy you and sell you and turn your life inside out if I choose."

"Billy!" The car swerved as Arlene half turned to stare at him, then she righted it, facing the front again, but angling the mirror so she could see him.

"You watch the road," he said. "I'm not finished. I heard more tonight about riffraff and rabble and rental slums than I have in all the past seventeen years. And let me tell you, I don't like it. I may have as much money as anybody on this Island now, but I was poor once, and I remember what it feels like. I remember the hopelessness, the struggle, the lack of dignity—being treated like dirt by the likes of you, Mrs. Hamilton! Poor people have as much right to live as the rich, and that's my prime reason for de—for wanting to see that development take place. It infuriates me to know that there are a lot of good people with their lives going to waste over there on the other side of that bridge and a lot of useless people over here on this side trying to stop progress for their own frivolous reasons!"

As he said it, he recognized it as the truth, and wondered where in the hell it had all come from, this sudden caring, this empathy with the Village and the people who lived there. Hell, his sole motive in planning the development had been revenge. In many ways, it still was, so where the hell did he get off going all soft and sentimental?

He didn't want to feel this way. He wanted to keep the sharp edge of hatred that had driven him all these years. Without that, what was he? Dammit, he'd given up booze. He'd given up dope. He'd given up womanizing. He'd even given up cigarettes, for God's sake! He wasn't about to give up everything that gave him pleasure. But he had to admit that what he'd heard tonight, coupled with what he'd seen in Oakmount over the course of the past month, really made him aware that the Village needed him as much as he needed it—as a means to achieve his famous revenge.

And now he didn't know where he sat, except on Arlene's hit list for upsetting the old dame in the front seat.

He sighed gustily and jammed both his hands into his hair, his elbows on his knees. "Oh, hell! I'm sorry, Mrs. Hamilton. Forgive my tirade."

"I forgive you nothing, Billy Culver. You're . . . scum, and you'll never be anything else. Money isn't the issue here, it's breeding, status, position . . ."

"Come along, Mrs. Hamilton," said Arlene gently, pulling up in the sweeping drive of the old and stately Hamilton home, and getting out to help the elderly lady out of the car. "Please don't upset yourself like this. I'm sure everything will work out in the end."

"Your father should never have sold that property, Arlene, and none of this would be happening. Oh, it's all such a shame. Such a shame . . ."

"I owe you an apology too," Billy said when Arlene returned to the car. He had moved into the front seat and turned the heater up another notch. It blew hot air across Arlene's face making her blink.

"Not really," she said with a tired sigh. "You were right and she was wrong. It's just that old habits die hard. In protesting what you said to her, I was simply doing what I'd have done if you'd attacked my grandmother."

"Don't worry about it," Billy said. "It's not the first time I've been told I don't belong. Or called a murderer because Curtis Hamilton took a dive into the rocks of Skyline Creek Canyon. It doesn't bother me."

Passion awaits you...
Step into the magical world of

Loveswept

E N J O Y . . .

PLUS **FREE GIFT**

tach and affix this stamp to the
reply card and mail at once!

Enjoy Kay Hooper's *"Larger Than Life"*!
Not for sale anywhere, this exclusive
novel is yours to keep—FREE—
no matter what!

S E E   D E T A I L S   I N S I D E . . .

A Magical World of Enchantment Awaits You When You're Loveswept!

Your heart will be swept away with Loveswept Romances when you meet exciting heroes you'll fall in love with...beautiful heroines you'll identify with. Share the laughter, tears and the passion of unforgettable couples as love works its magic spell. These romances will lift you into the exciting world of love, charm and enchantment!

You'll enjoy award-winning authors such as Iris Johansen, Sandra Brown, Kay Hooper and others who top the best-seller lists. Each offers a kaleidoscope of adventure and passion that will enthrall, excite and exhilarate you with the magic of being Loveswept

Enjoy 6 Romances–Risk Free! Plus...
An Exclusive Romance Novel Free!

Detach and mail card today!

Loveswept

Yes! *Please send my 6 Loveswept novels RISK FREE along with the exclusive romance novel "Larger Than Life" as my free gift to keep.*

AFFIX RISK FREE
BOOK STAMP
HERE.

RB   412 28

NAME

ADDRESS   APT.

CITY

STATE   ZIP

MY "NO RISK"
Guarantee

I understand when I accept your offer for Loveswept Romances I'll receive the 6 newest Loveswept novels right at home about once a month (before they're in bookstores!). I'll have 15 days to look them over. If I don't like the books, I'll simply return them and owe nothing. You even pay the return postage. Otherwise, I'll pay just $2.25 per book (plus shipping & handling & sales tax in NY and Canada). I save $3.00 off the retail price of the 6 books! I understand there's no obligation to buy and I can cancel anytime. No matter what, the gift is mine to keep–free!

SEND NO MONEY NOW. Prices subject to change. Orders subject to approval.

E N J O Y . . .

♥ 6 Romance Novels–Risk Free! ♥ Exclusive Novel Free!
♥ Money Saving Home Delivery!

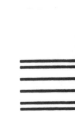

Arlene thought it did, but dropped the subject. "Where's Holly?"

"At home. Miss Quail stayed with her. I didn't know how late the meeting might run and didn't want to keep her up. How did she do with you this afternoon?"

Arlene smiled at the memory. "We had a good time. We talked about the new development, for one thing, and discussed how the meeting might go tonight. She agrees with me that a lot of the Islanders who object so strenuously are doing so out of fear of the unknown as much as elitism." She didn't tell Billy that they had also discussed several of the stories Holly had been told about her father during his youth, or that the child was quite impressed to have a genuine "ex-juvenile delinquent" for a daddy.

"I'm glad you agreed to help me with her," Billy said, taking her right hand off the wheel and spreading it on his leg. She snatched it back, too aware of his body heat through the fabric of his pants, the sleek, hard muscles of his leg, and what happened to her insides when that awareness struck. It lived now, too near the surface, ready at a moment's notice to reach out and strangle her breathing, heat her blood, pulse through every inch of her body.

"Hey," he said. "Don't be always pulling away from me, okay? I like to touch you."

"I don't like you to do it."

He laughed harshly. "Lord! I touched you the first night I was back, and baby, you loved it as much as I did."

She pulled to a halt in front of his cottage. "Billy, get off my back!"

His grin faded. "I'm not on your back, honey." He sighed, amazed at how tired he was all of a sudden—tired of her arguments, tired of waiting, tired of all the secrets, all the tensions, all the unasked questions and unspoken answers that lay between them like a thick, impenetrable curtain. Hooking a hand behind her head, he pulled her face to within inches of his and added softly, "But on your back is where I want you."

The breath escaped from her in a whoosh. Her eyes widened. Her lips parted. "Billy—"

"Ah, hell," he said, and then kissed her because there was nothing else he could do. She refused to respond, resolutely denied entrance to his probing tongue, remained completely still and passive even when he wrapped his other arm around her and hauled her up against his chest.

"Dammit, Arlie, will you kiss me?" He groaned in frustration. "Oh, baby, I need you tonight!"

"No," she said, planting her hands on his chest, trying desperately to ignore the hammering of his heart under her palms, the heat of his body, the hardness of his muscles. Not to mention the clamor of her own blood to do exactly as he demanded, as the scent of his skin and the rough timber of his voice appealed to her on several different levels. "No, Billy. Don't."

His eyes glittered between his lashes as he looked down at her. "Why not?"

"Because I don't want to," she lied, hoping it was dim enough in the car that he couldn't read her expression or see the rapid pulse in her throat.

His hold gentled as he searched her face in the light cast into the car by the single bulb over his porch. "Yes, you do, sweetheart," he said softly, touching that very pulse she'd worried about. "You want it as much as I do."

She said nothing, only looked at him, and part of him rejoiced to feel her heartbeat quicken. He cheered inwardly when she uttered no denial, made no attempt to escape his hold.

But another part of him trembled in fear. He knew, suddenly, that his need to touch her, to hold her, went right to the core of him. It was as elemental as air or water. It was a basic need of his, and he couldn't go on without it. It explained his sudden fierce joy when she'd spoken her approval of his development. It explained why he'd taken one look at her and decided to stay when all advice, even the advice of his own common sense, told him to go. It explained why he'd brought Holly to her when he hadn't needed to. It explained everything.

His gut clenched. This woman whose scent was so familiar, whose face had haunted his dreams for most of his life, and whom he had tried so hard to hate, was, had to be . . . *his*.

The intensity of his possessive feelings rocked him, and his hands tightened around her. His eyes squeezed shut, and he could scarcely contain the primitive howl that tried to rise up in his throat.

Her soft, breathy, "Billy . . . let me go" served only to inflame him. He looked down into her face again, drawing her toward him slowly, his gaze never leaving hers until her lids fluttered closed as if to shut out the sight of his face—or to lock away the flare of raw emotion in her eyes.

"I can't let you go," he said in quiet desperation. "I'm falling in love with you all over again, Arlie."

Her only response was to shiver and lean an inch closer to him, tilting her face up. "You mustn't!" she whispered. "Billy . . . *we* mustn't!"

He feathered tiny kisses over her lips, scarcely touching them. With the tip of his tongue he moistened her bottom lip, then outlined her top one, feeling it quiver under his sensual caresses. "But I am, darling. I have. So smooth, so sweet," he said. "I used to think about your sweet, innocent kisses, remember them, remember how they changed, quickly, Arlie, so quickly, from innocent to knowing, from tentative to yearning. Remember, baby? Remember how fast you learned?"

"I . . . remember." Her breath fanned his face, rapid, ragged. "Oh, Billy, stop." Her voice was a faint whisper, quavery with the passion she was trying to deny. He licked her upper lip once more, then her lower, and she moaned softly, parting her lips as if for more. Heartened by her involuntary response, he brushed light little kisses over her chin, up the bridge of her nose and along her throat. She made a small sound that was almost a word, but not one he wanted to hear her say. That one had sounded too close to no.

"Tell me yes," he said, placing more of the delicate, fluttering touches onto her lips until he burned with the need to deepen his kisses.

"Come to me," he murmured. "Show me how you feel. Is it there for you too? Are you falling in love with me all over again?"

"No." She moaned, and he didn't know if it was denial or refusal. He wouldn't believe a denial. He wouldn't permit her a refusal. Her eyes were closed, her face poised before him, lips parted, waiting, willing to let him take the lead, silently begging to be seduced. But that wasn't what he wanted of her this time.

"You're all grown up now, Arlie," he said, shaking her slightly. "Look at me. Show me what you feel."

"I don't know how."

"You do," he insisted. "I'm waiting. Open your eyes." With restraint that nearly killed him, he held back. He wanted her to want this as much as he did, and to admit it. Against his chest, her hands trembled. Her fingers curled and extended spasmodically as she kneaded his muscles, and he exulted deep within to know her need was growing apace with his. Her eyes were open, wide and dark gray, luminous

"I want you to . . . kiss me." The whisper was so soft, he wasn't absolutely certain he'd heard it. Her hands slid around his neck, drawing him down to her, and he responded with a rush of need.

Heat, perfumed by the scent of her skin, rose between them. He ran his hands into her hair, spreading it over the shoulders of her coat, burying his face in it before beginning a gentle assault of her mouth. When her breath was as ragged as his, her body trembling with the same kind of desire, he lifted his head and looked down at her face.

Her mouth was parted, moist from his tongue, from his lips. He watched her swallow, lick her lips, start to speak, then stop. Firming her suddenly trembling mouth, she looked at him as if she had a thousand secrets she was longing to share but didn't know where to begin.

Arlene shuddered with wanting as Billy bent his head toward her. His mouth moved over hers again, softly still, but with a subtly different demand, beseeching, now, beguiling rather than seducing. She nearly fainted from need. Hunger drove out judgment, negated every question she had ever been forced to ask over the years. She forgot the years, forgot the pain, because the pain of denying herself this pleasure was greater. With a deep sob of despair she kissed him back, sliding her arms around his neck, touching his thick hair, tasting him, breathing in his scent. She pulled his head down so that his mouth pressed harder, tighter to hers and she took what he gave, gave what he sought.

She didn't know she was weeping until he lifted his head and touched the wet tracks on her face.

"Arlie? What is it, sweetheart?" His tone was deep, compassionate, laced with tenderness. His dark brows formed a line across his forehead.

She tried to reply, but couldn't articulate a single word. All that came was another deep, hoarse sound of grief. She tried to move out of his arms, but he kept them around her, his hands stroking her hair and her back.

"Please, baby, stop it! Did I hold you too tight? Did I hurt you?"

She shook her head but couldn't stem the tears. They kept coming, and all she could do was bury her face against his chest, wrap her arms around his middle, and give in to her tearing, wrenching emotions while he held her, begging her to stop.

EIGHT

"Arlie, please, I can't stand to see you hurting like this! Tell me what it is, so I can make it better. I want to help."

But it was no good talking, he realized; she wasn't hearing him. He just held her, letting her cry until she was finished. Her breath came in little shuddering gasps, the way he remembered it doing when she'd cried with the abandon of childhood, the way Holly sometimes cried. Then, as he would with his daughter, he tilted her face up and looked at her ruined complexion. Arlene had never cried prettily. "Now," he said gruffly, "what brought that on?"

She evaded his gaze and pulled out of his embrace. "I . . . don't know. I'm sorry. Sometimes women get . . . emotional. You know that. I guess you caught me at a weak moment and . . . well, I maybe couldn't handle your . . . gentleness, or something."

Her evasions infuriated him suddenly. Dammit, whatever was happening to her was happening to him too. They both had a stake in this—whatever this was.

"Dammit!" he said rudely. "It wasn't gentleness you couldn't handle, Arlene! It was passion. I wasn't being kind. I was kissing the bejesus out of you, and you were doing exactly the same to me—making those wonderful little sounds in the back of your throat that tell a guy he's finally got it just right. Then the next thing I know, you're bawling. And I want to know what the hell brought it on!"

"I told you, I don't know!" she flared, rearing back from him. "It's been a long day and I'm worried about this new development and— Look, get out of my car now, will you, Billy? Go inside so I can go home. I'm tired."

"No damn way! I'm not leaving until I find out what the hell is going on with you!" he said stubbornly. "It's been driving me bananas trying to figure you out ever since I came back! What is it, Arlie? What's bothering you so much that you lie to me, lie to yourself, telling us both that you don't want me. This is me—Billy. I know you! I know you want me, and for some weird reason you're determined to fight it. Why, Arlene? Why?"

"You don't know me! You knew me a long time ago. I've changed. I . . . can't want you. I mustn't— we mustn't—do this again!"

He eyed her suspiciously. *Can't want you? We mustn't do this again?* What the hell?

He wanted to shake her. He wanted to yell at her. He wanted to . . . He blew out a long, angry, frustrated breath and forced himself to calm down. Yelling had never accomplished a damned thing, not in dealing with Arlene. He remembered a lot of things about her, and that was merely one of them.

"Why?" he asked again, but softly this time, his tone bewildered, his blue eyes probing her with a searching gaze. "Is it to do with where you go every weekend, Arlie? Is there someone . . . Hell!" The thought smacked him between the eyes. "Are you married?"

"No!" The word was jerked from her. He saw the panic in her face before she crossed her arms on the steering wheel and rested her head against them.

"Look at me," he said, but she could not. He saw

too much. He always had. He always would. He
was too perceptive where she was concerned. Of
course he'd noticed that she went away most weekends. And of course he wondered where she went.
But she could not, must not, tell him! He'd put it
all together and come up with the right answer, the
answer that would ruin several lives.

"You're not married." Somehow, he believed that,
though it would be easier to believe she was, that
she was locked into a marriage with somebody who
was in prison, or in a hospital or . . . he didn't know
what. But her denial was the truth.

"Tell me where you go, who you see," he asked
quietly. Whatever it was she did when she left the
island, it didn't make her happy.

She lifted her face and met his gaze. "I . . . can't
tell you that, Billy. It's a very personal matter and
it has nothing to do with you." Oh, God, another
lie! But what was one more when she considered all
the lies that had led up to that one?

His palm was large and warm on her nape. "Baby,
you never kept secrets from me before. Share this
with me, Arlie. Whatever it is, you can't handle it
alone. We both know that. I used to be your best
friend, and that's what best friends are for. For helping when we're hurting."

"We aren't best friends anymore," she said, but
he noticed she didn't deny the hurting. He also
noticed that her chin quivered just a bit and that she
blinked to force back a new rush of tears.

"Why not?"

"Because . . . we can't be." She frowned, silently
seeking his understanding. "Best friends are what
children have. And we're all grown-up."

With anyone else he might have left it at that,
shrugged, and got out of the car. But this was
Arlene, and maybe they were all grown-up, but
something in both of them would always respond

to the other as if they weren't. Sure, he'd come back to punish her. Then he'd seen her, and immediately he'd wanted to do something far different. Every time he'd seen her, that feeling had grown, and dammit, what he'd said earlier was true. He was falling in love with her again; now he wanted her even more. He wanted her for . . . for a long time, and he'd stopped thinking in "long" terms quite a while ago.

Until now.

The thought made him ache. God! Why did he have to *want* her so much? Why did it have to be her? She had lied to him, cheated him, and kept from him what was his because she was a Lambert. Maybe her grandparents were dead. Maybe she was an adult capable of making up her own mind, coming to her own decisions, but when it came right down to it, Lamberts did not marry their . . . servants.

He cocked his head to one side, looking at her speculatively. Was that it? Some kind of class guilt? She was a true Islander and he was an outsider, always had been, always would be. If she had a relationship with him, maybe she wouldn't be comfortable with her fellow Islanders.

Except . . . Arlene wasn't rich anymore. She was teaching kids who needed her. She was on-side with the Villagers on the boat yard issue. On-side with him, although she didn't know it. And she had kept his mother's things intact all those years. He continued to look at her, frowning.

"What is it? Why are you staring at me that way?"

He let out an explosive breath. "Why didn't you tell me about the cottage when you first learned it was mine?"

Her brows drew together. "We already discussed that. I told you why, Billy!"

"But you didn't tell me the truth," he accused.

"What makes you say that?"

"I just don't think you did." His gaze narrowed. "You were scared, weren't you? And that was why you didn't tell me." Fear leapt into her eyes, and he knew he'd hit it right on the button. But would she admit it? Hell, no! Not Arlene Lambert!

"Scared?" she scoffed. "What would I have to be scared of?"

"You tell me." When she didn't respond, he went on. "Okay, then, I'll tell you. You were afraid of exactly this." He touched her cheek, drew a line down her face to her throat and inside the collar of her coat, stopping when he reached the neck of her sweater. She shuddered delicately, and he knew it was not in distaste. "Afraid of what would rise up between us, within us, if I ever came back."

She drew in a tremulous breath and shifted away from him as far as the confines of the car permitted. "Billy . . . stop it. I'm begging you. Don't keep pushing me like this!"

"I have to," he said softly, sliding his hands down her arms, under them, around her waist inside her coat. "I can't let you get away with lying to us both the way you are."

But the truth would be so much worse for him! God! What am I supposed to do? Shatter his illusions? Tell him his mother had an affair with a married man—my grandfather? Tell him . . . ?

"No," she said both to herself and to Billy. "No. I can't. I won't."

"If you don't, I'll have to get the answers some other way, Arlie."

The tears she had been struggling with spilled over once more. "There are no answers!" she shouted. "God, Billy, if there were, I'd have found them years ago!"

"There must be. And this is one of them." He slid his arms fully around her and held her against him as he tipped her head back. His mouth was warm and demanding, and she didn't have any more hope of refusing him this time than she had the last. As they kissed, tongues darting, stroking, seeking, and finding, she wept softly, her tears running down to salt their lips.

"Ah, baby," he said moments later, lifting his head and wiping her face with his thumbs. "When I left you seventeen years ago, you were crying. It nearly killed me then, and it kills me now to see you in tears. Is that what it's all about? Because I took what you gave me and then didn't stay? Because I hurt you and you can't forgive me? Because you couldn't—can't—understand why I had to go?"

Her tears kept flowing. She touched his face with the palm of her hand, stroked his raspy chin, the smooth skin of his throat, tenderness inherent in every gesture. *Love*, he thought. There was love in her touch. It made his throat ache, his heart leap, and his body throb. If she loved him, why couldn't she admit it?

"No, Billy. I knew you had to go. And I knew why. That's why I wanted you to make love to me. So I'd have that much to remember. I didn't want you to stay. Not really. I understood."

"Then . . . are you unhappy because of Holly . . . and Sherril? Because you waited for me and I didn't wait for you?"

She sat erect, jerking herself free of him, forcing some stiffening into her spine. She smeared the tears from her face with the palms of her hands, searching for and finding a spurt of anger. The utter male arrogance of his question helped. "I never expected you back," she snapped. "I didn't *wait*. You actually believe that for seventeen years I've sat here moping over you? You have a highly inflated opinion of yourself, Billy Culver, just like you always had!"

"Oh. Right, you didn't wait. The venerable Sam and your famous engagement."

"There is no engagement, dammit! There was, but we broke it. However, Sam's willing to consider it on again anytime. All I have to do is tell him."

"Is that a threat?"

"Do I need to make threats to get a little peace from you?"

His eyes narrowed, and he glared at her. "You're not going to marry him, Arlene. Try it, and I promise I'll stop you."

"It's none of your business who I marry!"

"I'm making it my business." Once more he dragged her into his arms and pinioned her hands when she tried to fight. He kissed her hard until she became quiescent, then kissed her with all the gentleness he could muster. He stopped when she finally made a small, plaintive sound in her throat and leaned heavily against him. He touched her wild pulse again and eased her away from him, his loins aching. Damn, but she could make him hard like no other woman could!

"I'll stop you that way," he whispered. "I swear, if you try to marry him, I'll follow you right up to the altar and kiss you like that in front of the entire congregation. Nobody'd be surprised. Nobody'd try to stop me. It would only be what they'd expect of Billy Culver, acting like a jerk, showing off, screwing up other people's lives, butting in where he has no place. And when I flung you over my shoulder and marched out of the church with you, they'd all sit there on their stiff, rich asses and murmur politely that they all knew I'd come to no good."

Arlene drew in a tremulous breath and laughed. "Bad Billy Culver," she said. "I think you're beginning to believe your own press."

He opened the car door and grinned at her as the

dome light came on. "The thing is that *you'd* better start believing it."

"Oh, I do, I do," she said expansively with patent falseness, and started the engine again.

He gave her a hard look. "I need you to come in and stay with Holly while I drive Miss Quail home."

"You do, do you? After that little performance of yours, what makes you think I'll be willing to do what you want?"

He lifted his brows and grinned again. "I know you'd be horrified at the thought of my leaving an eight-year-old alone at night."

"You wouldn't!"

"Care to take the chance?"

"Damn you," she said, but turned off the key and got out of the car, accompanying him inside.

"Good night, Billy," Arlene said the moment he returned from having taken Miss Quail home. She had her coat on and her purse over her shoulder and stepped out the door before he had a chance to close it.

"Hey, wait a minute. What's the hurry?"

"I'm tired. Good night."

"I'll walk you home." He wrapped his fingers around her elbow.

"You can't leave Holly here all alone," she said reasonably, twisting her arm out of his clasp. She gave him a cheerful smile and ran down the steps. "Besides, what does that look like, sitting right there beside your car?"

"Oh." He shook his head. "Sorry. Stupid of me."

She gave him a long look and a nod of agreement and got into her car. It was only by exercising great restraint that she avoided showering his BMW with gravel in her tearing rush to get away. She didn't begin to relax until she was inside her house with the doors all locked.

Billy Culver had gotten too close tonight. She couldn't let it happen again.

"What the hell is going on?" Billy slammed the phone down. "I don't want to talk to you," he said, falsetto. "We have nothing to discuss, Billy." He kicked a hassock, then bent and rubbed his bruised toes. "Every damn day for a week, that's all I've gotten— 'We have nothing to discuss, Billy.' "

"What's that, Daddy?"

"Nothing," he barked. "Go brush your teeth and get ready for school."

"My teeth are brushed and I'm ready. I'm waiting for you to drive me there."

Billy sighed gustily. "Right. Let's go."

"Aren't you going to get dressed, Daddy?"

He looked down at his bare feet and legs sticking out from under his velour bathrobe and said, "No. As a matter of fact, I'm not. I'm going this way."

Shoving his feet into a pair of loafers, he grabbed his keys from the table in the hall and held open the front door for his bug-eyed daughter. Together they walked to the car, Holly casting sidelong glances at him all the way.

"You know," she said as the car rolled onto the bridge, "I think it's kind of neat, having a juvenile delinquent for a dad. Like you're some kind of a hero."

He was startled. "Who told you that about me?"

"Oh, everyone. Arlie said it's true, and that you really did make moonshine at school and paint the principal's car black and orange on Halloween after he suspended you."

Billy scowled, remembering. "He didn't suspend

me. He kicked me out. Totally. Forever." He pulled a face. "Being a juvenile delinquent isn't all it's cracked up to be, so don't go making a hero of me."

"That's what Arlie said. She said getting into all that trouble didn't make you happy, and that you got into most of it because you were very unhappy. Are you happy now, Daddy?"

He ran a hand over his unshaven face. "Sure, babe." He wasn't sure she'd buy it. She didn't.

"You don't look happy. And you're grouchy. And you're out of the house in your bathrobe in broad daylight." She eyed him thoughtfully for several seconds. "I think you did that because you wanted to break a rule this morning."

He swallowed hard, wishing he didn't have such a perceptive kid. "And if I did? Is it such a bad rule to break?"

"No, but the point is, why did you want to break one? What's eating you, Daddy?"

"A guy's just got to work out some things for himself, even when he has a resident genius on hand who probably has all the answers."

After a moment, looking worried, she shrugged. "Okay, whatever you say. Like you tell me, I can't force you to talk. But you know, you could always ask Arlie to help you find the answers. She's really smart and she never, ever lies. There might be times she refuses to answer, but if she tells me something, I know it's the absolute truth."

Arlene? Truth? Rage began to build in his chest. Sure, Arlene never, ever lied. Except to him. "Yeah. Right," he said heavily, pulling up in front of the school and leaning over to open the door for her. "Now, you scoot, chickie. Oops, there goes the bell."

"Bye, Daddy!" Holly gave him a loud, smacking kiss on the cheek and hopped out of the car, running up the front steps of the school, her golden-brown hair bouncing on the back of her neon pink and orange jacket.

For several moments Billy sat, thinking over her words, fury churning in his gut along with hurt and something else he refused to define but hated himself for feeling. Arlene never lied to Holly, not even to protect *him*. What the hell kind of friend was she anyway? Did she have to tell his own innocent daughter that he'd been nothing more than a dirty little punk as a kid? A juvenile delinquent? Couldn't she have denied the old stories, shown him in a better light? Sure, of course she could have. She had chosen not to! To get back at him. Did he really want such a two-faced, disloyal, cheating woman teaching his child?

It ate at him, gnawing a big, raw hole inside him. Of course that was how she still saw him! As the housekeeper's son, not good enough for a Lambert. It probably accounted for her refusal to talk to him, to see him, to have anything to do with him ever since that night they'd got carried away in the car.

Was she afraid if she let herself go again, she'd end up behind the rhododendron bushes making love to one of the servants?

"Oh, damn her to hell and back!" he ground out, slamming the transmission into reverse and gunning the BMW out of the school driveway—right into the side of a cement truck crawling slowly up the hill.

"That was my sister Gail," said June, hanging up the phone in the kitchen. She'd answered it because Arlene's hands were coated to the elbow with papier-mâché guck. "Guess what's going on right outside her classroom window?" June was hardly able to contain her laughter.

"What?" Arlene was in a hurry to get back to her small class.

"Billy Culver, in his skivvies, directing traffic around the wreckage of his car and a cement truck."

Arlene's papier-mâché landed in the sink with a splat. "What?" she said again, this time with horror-widened eyes. "Was Holly with him? Are they all right? His *skivvies*?"

"Well, not exactly skivvies, but his bathrobe and nothing else. Holly's fine. He'd just dropped her off when he backed out real fast, smack into the side of the cement truck. I guess Billy didn't see the thing, though I wonder how he could miss something that size."

Arlene wondered more about why he had driven Holly to school dressed in nothing more than a bathrobe, but determinedly put it out of her mind as she went back to her class.

It didn't stay out of her mind long, however. Not half an hour later, after her door suffered three sharp raps, it swung open and banged against the wall. Billy was there, his long, hairy legs with knobby knees sticking out from under a white-piped navy bathrobe. His black loafers and their little tassels were wet with mud and, probably, cement. His eyes were cold, his lips were blue, and his fists were clenched at his sides.

"I want to talk to you," he said. "Right now."

"Billy, I have a class in session," she said pleasantly, forcing a smile. None of these children could deal adequately with stress. That was why they were in this sheltered environment. "Shut the door quietly on your way out, please. I'll have a visit with you later." They must not think Billy was a threat to her; she was their security. Anything that endangered her endangered them.

He moved in on her, towering over her, oblivious to the alarmed stares of the children, the concerned face of Arlene's teaching assistant. "Arlene, I'm warning you. You come with me willingly, or you come with me unwillingly. One way or the other, you are coming with me."

"Billy, please be reasonable. Would you like to visit with the class for a few minutes? Boys and girls, this is Mr. Culver. He's an old friend of mine. Can you all say 'Good morning, Mr. Culver'?"

No one said a word, but Stevie Austin let out a wail of terror and hid under a table. Kathy Brodgisil wet her pants, and Ethan Crandall started a rhythmic flapping of his hands as Billy picked Arlene up and swung her over his shoulder, then strode out the door and slammed it shut behind him.

NINE

He didn't stop for anything or anyone until he had walked through the pouring rain with her all the way to his cottage. There, he dumped her onto the couch and glared down at her.

"What," he said, "do you mean by telling my daughter that I was a juvenile delinquent?"

"Are you completely out of your mind?" she said, leaping to her feet and shoving him hard, her palms slamming into his chest. She might as well have tried to push that cement truck he'd bashed into.

"I didn't tell her that, but when she asked me if what other people were saying was true, I had to tell her it was. If I'd tried to whitewash you, she'd have caught on at once. You know that! Nobody can put things over on Holly. Nobody who wants her trust should ever try! I promised her the first day we talked that she could ask me anything about any subject and get an honest answer from me. If you don't like the way I'm handling my part of her education, then replace me. But if you ever, ever again interrupt me when I have a class in progress, then I will call in the law. And that, Billy Culver, is God's own truth!

"Do you have the faintest idea of what you've accomplished this morning? You have wiped out the effects of nearly five months of careful work. Those children in my class are *disturbed*, Billy! Their emotions and psyches are delicate and fragile! They are beginning to learn to trust me. Anything out of the ordinary, any upset of any kind, is so stressful to most of them that it'll take me weeks to regain the lost ground. Oh, dammit, I don't have time to stay here and tell you what you've done. I have to get the hell back there and try to undo it!"

With that, she shoved past him and out the door—as unconcerned about the rain as he had been when he'd carried her from her house. She was so mad it was a wonder she didn't steam all the way home. But she managed to get her temper in hand before going back to her kids.

It took the rest of the day to bring order to her room, and she was exhausted by the time Holly arrived. She stood looking at Holly, seeing that she had been crying and wondering if there was enough strength within her to deal with whatever crisis Holly was suffering. She reached out a welcoming hand. "Come on in and tell me what's wrong."

Holly's face was a mask of misery. "I can't. I just came to say that D-Daddy asked Miss Quail to teach me after school because he doesn't like you anymore. He wasn't going to tell you, Arlie, but I said if he didn't let me do it, then I wouldn't go to Miss Quail's." Tears flowed freely from her eyes and her mouth twisted as she sobbed. "I don't want to go to Miss Quail's! I want to stay with you and when I told him he got mad and he didn't even wink!"

"Oh, sweetheart, don't cry!" Arlene pulled Holly inside and shut the door. She gathered her into her arms and took her to a sofa, where she sat holding her on her lap. Damn Billy! Damn him for acting like a jerk again! He'd done this to his child because he was mad at *her*! "Listen, it'll be okay. Miss Quail is a wonderful teacher. When your dad first asked me to teach you, my instinct was to suggest her instead, but somehow that never happened."

"I . . . don't . . . wa-ant . . . her!" Holly could barely speak, she was crying so hard. "I want you." Holly wept, her face buried against Arlene's bosom. "You have to talk to him, Arlie. You have to!"

"Darling, I can't." Arlene smoothed Holly's hair back from her face. "The decision is his. It would be terribly wrong of me to interfere between the two of you. You can understand that, can't you?"

"No! No!" Holly shook her head wildly from side to side. "Sometimes . . . sometimes, we need someone to intervene. Mostly M-Mavis. Oh, Arlie, I miss Mavis so mu-uh-uh-uch. I love her and I want to go home! If I can't be with you, then I want to be with her."

There was nothing Arlene could say. All she could do was offer silent comfort to this heartbroken baby who was catching all the fallout from her father's inexplicable fit of temper and completely unable to understand why.

"Holly! Hey, sugar plum, what's keep— Oh, shi . . . oot!" Billy came to halt, taking in the scene in Arlene's living room.

He smacked his forehead with the heel of one hand and whispered, "Oh, my Lord, what have I done?"

"I don't know," said Arlene, glaring at him. "But I suggest you undo it, pal, and fast."

Billy chewed on his lower lip as he listened to his daughter sob over and over, "I want to go home to Mavis."

"Sweetheart, don't cry like that," he said, crouching before Arlene and Holly. His hand hovered over his daughter's hair as if he wanted to touch her but was afraid. "I'm sorry. I blew up over nothing. I was wrong and it wasn't your fault at all. I was mad at Ar—at someone else and—"

"Yoo-ou didn't wuh-wuh-wink, Daddy!"

"Baby, I know. I forgot. Come here. Come to Daddy," he begged, but Holly clung to Arlene, shaking her head.

"Time out, Daddy," she said. "Please. Time out."

Billy raised anguished eyes to Arlene, silently asking for help. There was none she could offer. This was his baby. All at once she was fiercely glad that he hadn't been around to father her baby, the lousy, insensitive, clumsy lout! He didn't deserve a wonderful little girl like Holly! And for sure he didn't deserve ever, ever to know about Marcy, no matter how much she was sometimes tempted to tell him and damn the consequences.

"Can she stay?" he said finally, getting to his feet.

"Of course. It's time for our session anyway." Arlene's voice sent chills down his spine. Her eyes, with their fierce, protective anger, reminded him of a lynx he'd once seen standing between her young and a badger. God, what a waste that she had no children! Suddenly, he wished with all his heart that Holly was *theirs*. He swallowed hard, nodded, and with a last, yearning look, went out quietly.

When he returned at six-thirty, Arlene met him at the door, her gray eyes darkly bleak, her shoulders drooping with weariness. "Why don't you leave her with me, Billy? Just for the night. She's sleeping now and calm." Her voice was flat and emotionless, as if every ounce of feeling had been drained from her soul.

His relief was palpable. He felt his knees start to sag and grasped the edge of the doorway. They needed a time-out, he and Holly. His daughter was right about that.

"Sure, she can stay the night, as long as everything is all right between the two of us again. This isn't the first time I've screwed things up with Holly. Sometimes we clash. Something got to me, and I let myself blow up. It had nothing to do with her, but she got the flack, and I forgot to give her our special signal that tells her I'm just mad, but not mad at her." He pulled a face. "Oh, hell, I may as well be truthful. I didn't forget. I couldn't wink at her because in a way I *was* mad at her—only it was damned unreasonable, I shouldn't have been."

"She loves you, Billy, and you can hurt her pretty badly when you cut loose with that temper of yours."

"I know." He looked humble, contrite. "Arlie, I love that little girl more than I can tell you. She's my life. That's not something a person who isn't a parent can fully understand. Look, if she's going to stay, can I stay too?"

Her eyes reflected her shock. "For the night?"

"No, no, of course not," he said quickly, then with a twisting smile, added, "Ah, hell, why not be truthful about that too? Yes, I'd like to stay for the night, for every night for the rest of my life."

Her stomach leapt and flopped like a landed fish, and it was not a comfortable feeling. Neither was the wave of guilt she felt because his words made her react that way. God, what kind of a perverted soul was she?

"No," she said flatly.

"Hell, I'm not stupid. I know you won't let me stay the night. But for the evening? I could go over to the Village and get pizza or Chinese or whatever you want. I just want to be close to Holly." *And you.*

"No," she said again, fighting the desire to tell him yes, to have dinner with him, to curl up and talk, to share with him every one of those long, difficult seventeen years they'd been apart. That one evening they'd spent talking over dinner, and later over coffee by the fire, hadn't been nearly enough.

He sighed. "All right, then. But let me see her. I won't wake her up. I just want to kiss her good-night so that she knows, inside, that everything's all right. May I?"

She stood back, gesturing toward the stairs. "She's your child, Billy, so of course you can see her. But everything is not all right, let me tell you. She thinks you're mad at her for being interested in your youth and is also very unhappy that you brought her here, away from everyone who's familiar to her. I've explained that it wasn't her you're mad at, but me. Only I couldn't tell her why because I don't know myself."

Billy sighed and leaned against the door. "You want me to tell you." It was a statement, not a question.

"It might help."

"Help who?"

"All of us."

He shook his head. "It sure as hell hasn't helped me, Arlene." His mouth twisted. "All right, if you have to know, I saw red because Holly was extolling your laudable truthfulness. She said you promised never to lie to her and that you haven't. Yet you lie to me all the time, and I hate it! Dammit, you were my friend *first*! I feel like an outsider again when the two of you are together. You shut me out. I—oh, hell, I feel like a ten-year-old with injured feelings!" He turned from her, his head drooping. He sounded ashamed. "I know I'm acting like one, too, but I feel so damned betrayed because you keep the truth from me!"

She could have cried with the agony in her chest, with the need to tell him the things she was keeping from him. But she could not.

Drawing in a deep, steadying breath, she said quietly, "Billy, what have I lied to you about?" *Is not telling you everything the same as lying?* She knew it was, in anybody's book, but there was nothing she could do about it.

He turned to confront her again, his face drawn, his eyes tired. "I don't know. Not really. I just know that you have, you are. Because you're fighting your need for me as hard as I once fought mine for you. But at least I admit the feelings are still there, or there again—or whatever the hell it is going on with you and me."

Squaring her shoulders, she steeled herself and looked him right in the eye. "There is nothing going on with you and me. There can never be anything between us, Billy. And that is the truth. I swear it. If Holly were to ask me, that's what I would tell her. You and I are a dead issue. Case closed."

He looked at her for a long time, reading the determination in her eyes, then nodded, feeling sick with repressed anger, burning with the need to make her hurt as badly as she made him hurt.

"Mind if I use your phone?"

"Of course not."

He leafed through the directory on the hall table, then picked up the phone and dialed quickly. With a glance at her, he said, "Hi, Ellen. How'd you like to come out to the Island and pick me up? My car's out of commission, but since I have an unexpected baby-sitter tonight, I don't want to waste a free evening. Right. Soon. Oh, and ring Arlene's place when you get here. She'll buzz the gate open for you. I don't have mine connected yet."

He hung up and smiled at Arlene, glad to see that what little color had been in her face was drained. She looked every day of her thirty-four years. She was tired and aching . . . and so damned ethereally beautiful he wanted to have her right there. If he hadn't experienced the power of her adamant rejection, he'd go for it and let Ellen ring and ring and never get an answer. If he could have Arlene, the gate could stay locked against Ellen and everyone else forever.

Instead, he said, "You don't mind, do you?"

She met his gaze. "No. Not in the least. Have a nice time."

"Thank you," he said. "I intend to have a *great* time. Good night."

"Good night."

Without looking at Arlene again, he strode out, closing the door softly behind him. She wondered if he even cared that he'd forgotten to kiss Holly good-night. No, the man was not a good father, she told herself. For two cents, she'd take Holly and run.

What are you thinking? she asked herself, slumping onto the couch and burying her face in her hands. *Holly isn't even your child!* But, oh, how she wished it were so. What kind of a woman was she, who wanted a man's children but didn't want the man?

She leaned her head back and laughed. Didn't want the man? Who was she trying to kid anyway? She laughed again, surprised to discover that her face was wet with tears, that the internal ache had found a release in deep, irrepressible sobs that even the sofa cushions couldn't muffle completely.

"They're becoming a real item, aren't they?" Sam looked smug and complacent as he lifted his glass and sipped, watching Arlene's eyes as if to assess her feelings over the "they" he'd commented on.

She gave him a careful, bland look. "I suppose they could be." From the moment they'd arrived, she'd been as aware as Sam that Billy and Ellen were seated on a banquette toward the back of the restaurant, very close together, talking and laughing intimately.

She told herself it didn't matter, but it hurt just as much as when Billy had used her phone to call Ellen that night nearly two weeks before. Still, as long as Billy didn't know it hurt her, she was sure she could deal with it. "Have they been seeing a lot of each other?"

"Oh, a great deal, according to Ellen," said Sam, answering the question she had asked without really wanting to hear a reply. "He's even moved a big motor home onto his property adjacent to the cottage so they can have a place to meet privately. I can tell you that much without breaking any professional confidences, since she's boasted about it to anyone who'll listen."

"Oh. I understood that the motor home was because his housekeeper from Phoenix has come to live with them here. The cottage only has two bedrooms."

"Be that as it may, it isn't the housekeeper who sleeps in the motor home, but Billy."

And Ellen, Sam didn't say, but the words echoed through Arlene's mind as if he had. His eyes cut to Billy. Arlene's followed, against her will, and lingered. Billy was now leaning closer than ever to Ellen, his hand rubbing slowly up and down her side as they talked, skimming past the side of her breast. Even from a distance Arlene could see that Ellen's large nipples were erect below the low-cut front of her thin silk dress. She slid her fingers under Billy's tie, inserting them between the buttons of his shirt. Arlene wanted to scream.

"Look at him." Sam's nose wrinkled. "Look at *them.* Animals. Two of a kind, touching each other like that in public, all over each other!"

Arlene's smile felt ghastly on her face. "If it offends you, Sam, why look? Shall we go now? I'd enjoy a good long walk."

Last night's walk had only whetted her appetite, Arlene thought the next morning, waking early. It

was Sunday, and she should be in Seattle with
Marcy. But a pressing fear that Billy might have
her followed, or even follow her himself, had
made her phone the school with a message that
she couldn't make it. She had gone the week
before, feeling safe because Billy was in Phoenix
helping Mavis pack.

Marcy would understand. She knew her mother
couldn't come every weekend, and besides, there
were times Marcy herself was busy and she and
Arlene didn't get together.

"But I miss her," Arlene said aloud. "Why am I
letting Billy do this to us? And what am I going to
do if he never leaves?" Those were not questions
for which she had answers, and she wondered if
she ever would.

Dressed in warm slacks and a lined jacket, she
tugged on a pair of leather gloves and ran down the
trail to the beach, jumping over the silver logs and
drawing in the pungent scents of salt and grass and
seaweed. In spite of the nippy air, spring had nearly
arrived. Crocuses, daphne, and Cape jasmine were
already in bloom, and daffodils hung fat, heavy
heads in prayer for the sunny days that would make
them open.

The raw wind chilled her. She started out on her
walk at a fast pace and soon warmed up. As she
scrambled over the rocks at the base of the hill that
separated the south end of the Island from the
north, she wondered with a twinge of sadness how
many more times she would be able to walk this
way. Soon, construction of the boat yard would
begin and this section of shore would be lost to the
Islanders.

According to the previous day's newspaper, the
ecological studies for the new development were
complete, final permissions had been granted, and
everything was a go. Even most of the opposition

on the Island had died down to a dull series of grumbles.

As she crossed the foreshore in front of Admiral Forsythe's house, he waved to her. She waved back, then stopped when she saw him hurrying down the shore to intercept her.

"Arlene, I've been trying to reach you!" He was puffing, his face red from exertion and, she soon saw, from fury. "I saw that your car was there when I was on my way home from church, but you refused to answer your door or your phone. I understand that, though. You must be heartily ashamed to show your face among your friends and neighbors!"

"Admiral!" She gaped at him, shocked almost speechless. "What—"

He shook his fist at her. "Don't you interrupt me, young lady! Your grandmother taught you better manners than that! How would she feel about all this?" He waved his walking stick in a threatening manner, describing an arc near Arlene's nose. "She'd find your actions inexcusable, unforgivable, *reprehensible*, as do the rest of us! How could you have permitted this to happen, young woman? No, more than permitted, encouraged!"

"Permitted what to happen?" Lord, he looked as if he were about to collapse from apoplexy! "Admiral, I don't understand what I've done."

Planting his stick on a silvery beach log and leaning his two hands on top of it, the admiral continued, his rheumy blue eyes narrowed as he glared at her. "Oh, you understand, all right! And to think we all trusted you. We listened to you when you said we should stop objecting. You told us we should be good neighbors and give the newcomers a chance. You claimed that times have changed— that no one group can hope to hold exclusive title to an entire island forever. Your grandfather, rest his soul, would disown you for what you've done!"

The boat yard? The old man was blowing his stack about the boat yard again? And here she'd thought it was all over. All over but the shouting, it seemed, and Admiral Forsythe still needed to do some of that. Well, dammit, she'd had enough. He could quit shouting at her, for starters. Drawing herself up to her full height, she stared him right in the eye.

"Excuse me," she said, "but with all due respect, I must point out that I have done nothing, Admiral Forsythe. I'm not the one who sold that property. That, as you might recall, was my father, and I resent being blamed for it."

"Oh, yes, it was your father who started this entire sellout, this giveaway, this deplorable undermining of the very fabric of our society on this island. But it was *you*, young miss, who encouraged that boy, treated him as if he were an equal, gave him ideas above his station. Now look what's happened! He's bought every acre of what was once the glory of your grandfather's estate. He's going to cut down all the trees, tear up the beaches, and turn the land into a Dogpatch. A Dogpatch, I tell you, Arlene, and you could have stopped it!"

She stared at him. "Boy? What boy?"

"What boy?" he bellowed. "What boy did you always pander to? What boy was allowed to get away with murder because of your grandfather's soft-headedness toward him? What boy did you spend your girlhood lollygagging with when you should have been preparing yourself for marriage to someone from your own strata?"

"Billy?" Arlene stared at the old man disbelievingly. "Are you talking about Billy Culver?"

He lashed at a defenseless, stiffly cold wild rosebush with his cane. Arlene jumped back. "And who else would I be talking about? Of course Billy Culver! That upstart! That overgrown guttersnipe! That— And you were in cahoots with him! I want you off my property, miss. I wish never to see your face again. You have allied yourself with the wrong elements once too often for my liking. Good day."

With one final slash at the bush, the admiral wheeled away with correct military precision and marched toward his large, lonely home, his back stiff, his shoulders squared. His fury seemed to linger in the chill air.

"Billy?" Arlene whispered. "I don't believe it."

But she did. Sadly, strangely, emptily, she did. And in a funny kind of way, it all made sense.

TEN

Arlene hammered on the door of Billy's motor home. She didn't care if she was waking him up as Mavis had warned her. She had to talk to him, and she had to do it right now!

"This is a surprise," he said when he finally came to the door. His hair was tousled. His face was unshaven. He had bags beneath his eyes. He wore a pair of half-zipped jeans low on his hips and nothing else. He looked like a million dollars. "What can I do for you?"

With difficulty, Arlene averted her gaze from his powerfully muscled chest, his rippled abdomen, the half-open zipper. Either he wore very skimpy briefs, or nothing at all under his jeans. She swallowed hard and snapped, "I want to talk to you about that boat yard, Billy Culver!"

Suddenly, he looked wary. "What about it?"

"What *about* it!" she yelled, pushing past him into the warmth of his motor home. "It's yours, that's what about it! And now half the Islanders think I was in on the deal with you all along!" She tore off her leather gloves and slapped them on the edge of the table for emphasis. "Nobody believes that I knew nothing about it! Damn you, Billy, what right did you have to put me in this position?" She flung

147

her coat and scarf onto a settee, threw her hat on top of them, and whirled on him with her last question.

He laughed.

Arlene wanted to hit him with something hard, something heavy, something blunt. How could he stand there laughing while her reputation in the community hung in shreds at her feet?

"So," he said, shutting the door of the motor home. It closed with a solid, expensive thunk that Arlene hated herself for noticing. "It's finally hit the fan, has it? I wonder who did the digging."

"Gunther Nelson!" she spat out.

"The editor?"

"Exactly! And he couldn't wait for his Wednesday edition to publish his big scoop. He made a public announcement in church this morning! Dammit, why didn't you come clean? Why the secrecy? Why hide behind an agent, a corporation, a smokescreen of functionaries? If you wanted to destroy the Island, why not come right out and do it openly?"

"Oh, so now my boat yard is going to 'destroy the Island'?" He leaned against the counter, crossing his arms, looking down his nose at her. "Now that you know it's mine, it's destructive, is it? Yet when it was some unknown developer's, it was good for Oakmount Village. It was going to provide much-needed employment, and housing that even the poor could afford, and that was good. Typical Island logic. If Billy Culver's got a hand in it, it's gotta be bad. And you ask why I didn't tell anyone?"

"I'm not asking why you didn't tell anyone. I'm asking why you didn't tell me! *Retired*, you said! Oh, sure. And I believed it! Why? Why would I believe such an obvious crock? I'm a sucker for your stories, aren't I, Billy? That's why you knew you could get away with it! Because I've always been a sucker for you. Well, no more, friend! I'll never believe another thing you tell me! God, Billy, and all the times you accused me of lying, you were lying even bigger, even better than I've ever dreamed of doing! How could you do this? Couldn't you at least have told *me*? What about that friendship of ours you keep harping on?"

He stared at her sullenly. "You're the one who kept denying that friendship, saying it was a dead issue, that our case was closed. So why should I have told you anything?" He sat down at the table, swiveling one of the captain's chairs away from her and placing his elbows on his knees, his head in his hands.

"Go away, Arlene. I was up late and I'm tired and have a headache. I don't want to listen to you yelling at me."

"Hung over, I suppose?" she asked nastily.

He lifted his head and looked at her. "I don't drink." His answer surprised her, but not as much as his next statements. "The strongest drug I use is caffeine. I'm a recovering alcoholic. I belong to AA. Hell, I even quit smoking three years ago. Except for the night I came back here. Then I smoked three of the damn things. You drove me to it, Arlene. You!"

She stared silently at him for several moments, trying to read his unreadable eyes, wondering if she could believe that—any of it. She remembered the hard-drinking youth he'd been, and remembered too, that dinner she'd shared with him and Holly. That night Billy had drunk milk. He'd put brandy in her coffee. Had he put any in his?

A coffee maker stood on the counter by twin stainless sinks. She filled its reservoir, scooped in coffee from the can beside it, and switched it on. It gurgled to life while she searched out two cups, sugar and cream. When the coffee was ready, she filled the cups, holding her hand as steadily as she could. She set the cream and sugar out along with one spoon. She drank hers black.

So, she saw, did Billy. That, too, was a change. Once, he'd used three spoons of sugar and more cream than he was entitled to. She lifted her brows in question.

"When caffeine's the strongest substance in a guy's life, he doesn't want to dilute it with anything." He sipped, watching her.

They both remained silent until he said heavily, "Would you have been so willing to talk on the side of the development if you'd known I was behind it?"

Without hesitation, glaring at him angrily, she said, "Yes. Because it's a good development. And it will benefit the Village." Her glare faded to a frown. She looked at the table, traced a pattern with the handle of the spoon, then glanced up at him, apologetic.

"What I said, about your ruining the Island . . . well, that was a direct quote from Dr. Gray. He called this morning—so did most of my grandparents' old friends. They all seem to think I've sold out. But what I said, about what it will do for the Village, I meant that, Billy. The whole thing is well planned. Somebody did a lot of advance thinking."

"Me," he said. "Over quite a few years." He grinned, but there was more bitterness in it than humor. "The day I learned that the cottage was mine, I started dreaming of a big, bad payback, something to hurt you, Arlene. And the others."

"Hurt me, I could understand. But the others? Why them?"

He sighed and sipped his coffee. "Because they treated me like dirt too many times. I wanted to pay the Island back."

"And in the process, do something nice for the people who had accepted you? The Village."

He shot her a look, half annoyed, half amused. "I didn't see it that way. Not at first. Sherril was the one who pointed out the other side of the coin. I told her I didn't give a damn about Oakmount Village."

"You did, though, didn't you? I mean, you couldn't have come up with anything better designed to benefit the Village. What you proposed was so perfect, the council had no choice but to accept it and promote it."

He shrugged and looked uncomfortable. Billy Culver was no Boy Scout, and he resented people thinking he was acting like one. "When I bought that land, I spent a lot of sleepless nights thinking up things I could do with it that would irk the Islanders, cause them to tear out their hair." He grinned again, this time with genuine amusement.

"I thought of a resort catering to Hell's Angels, something like that. Then I figured maybe a mushroom-growing operation." His grin became a chuckle. "You know what mushrooms are grown in."

Arlene had to smile, but she killed it quickly. Where was this leading? He wasn't answering anything she wanted to know. "Billy—"

"No, let me finish. Then I considered a fish farm, but the water's too shallow. I love all the controversy over the aquaculture industry. It's a real battle of the haves against the have-nots. A fish-processing plant would have been a good revenge, too, but like the mushroom operation, the stink would have caused me as much trouble as it did anyone else. I like the smell of fresh ocean breezes as well as the next guy. Anyway, I had a lot of years to think and scheme and plot."

She frowned. "Wait a minute. When, exactly, did you buy that land?"

"Nine years ago—when it was offered to me. That's how I learned your grandfather had left the cottage to my mother. I was a registered landowner of Oakmount Island and entitled to bid on the land."

She stared at him, remembering how, all those years before, everyone had assumed that no buyer had been found. Yet one had. Billy Culver. And they had not been given a chance to approve or disapprove of him because he was legally an Island property owner already and didn't require anyone's approval. No wonder the Islanders blamed her, or at least her family. She bit her lip and shook her head slowly. What a mess! What a terrible, ungodly mess, and there was nothing she could do to change it!

"What are you thinking?"

"That none of this would have happened if my grandfather hadn't gambled away his fortune."

"And that it's bitterly ironic that his housekeeper's son bought the property in the end?"

"No," she said, offended. Did he have to assume she was such a snob? What had she ever done to him—that he knew about—except fail to tell him the cottage was his? That, she supposed, was enough. "I wasn't thinking about that at all, and I resent your suggestion! But it was lucky for you that you had the cottage, wasn't it? None of the old-timers would have given their approval of your 'morals and social position.' I wonder why so many people feel that social position guarantees good morals and acceptable behavior?" She thought about her grandfather and his affair with Billy's mother, and was glad he didn't know.

Billy shrugged. "Who knows." He, too, was thinking about his mother and her affair with Arlene's grandfather. No matter what, he was glad Arlene knew nothing of that old, sordid story. He'd hate her to know. She'd adored both her grandparents. If it had ever become public, the Lambert family name would have taken a hell of a beating.

"So you waited for nine years to do what you'd planned. And to come back." She didn't know if she was glad or sad that he'd waited so long. In a way, it was better like this. She'd had those nine years to finish recovering, to gain strength, to stop blaming herself entirely for events over which she had no control.

"That's right. It took everything I had to buy the land and a hell of a lot I didn't have. I was mortgaged up to my, uh, eyeballs. So I had to start pretty much from scratch again in order to afford the kind of development I wanted for the island."

"It can't have been easy."

"It wasn't, Arlie." He grinned. "But the second fortune comes easier. Though not a hell of a lot."

"S&H," she said. "What does it stand for, Sherril and Holly?"

He smiled faintly, shaking his head. "No, though I guess most people would think so. Actually, I named my company before I married Sherril and long before we'd even chosen the name Holly." His smile deepened to a devilish grin. "A good friend told me that if I was going into business, I needed a company name that meant something to me, something that would serve as inspiration to keep me going when things were tough. So I named it for two things I'd raised a lot of all my life."

Arlene thought about it for a second and then laughed softly. "I don't suppose you're talking about sugar and hay."

He shook his head, reaching out to clasp her wrists, drawing her off her chair until she knelt between his knees.

"I love to hear you laugh like that," he said, cupping her head in his hands, bending his face toward hers, his breath warm on her cheeks. "I love the way you understand me. I love—"

He broke off as the door slammed open and Holly darted in, her face flushed, her hair all over, her eyes wide and full of awe. "Daddy! Arlie! Come quick! Come and see! It's snowing!"

"My dear, I would like to apologize. May I come in?"

Arlene stood back, swinging the door wide for Admiral Forsythe. "Of course. But there's no need to apologize. I can sympathize with your feelings." She closed the door on the wet, whipping wind. The snow of three days before had gone within twenty-four hours, succumbing to a driving rain that had not let up since.

With a courtly gesture that stopped short of being a bow, the admiral handed her a huge box, which she knew would contain prize roses from his greenhouse. "There is every need. I was unforgivably rude and made quite unfounded accusations."

Arlene opened the box and lifted out the dozen long-stemmed American Beauties. "How lovely!" She smiled at him. "Thank you, Admiral. A handsome apology, which I accept with pleasure."

"Then my pleasure is doubled," he said with another stiff little bow. Arlene stood staring after the upright old figure, wondering what had happened to change his opinion of her.

Dr. Gray phoned an hour later, also with an apology, then two more Islanders after him. When Kevin Morrison II called, she finally asked what was going on. He was of her generation and she felt comfortable questioning him.

"Oh, early yesterday Billy called on the admiral and asked him to set up a meeting of the Island Property Owners' Association," he told her.

"Really?" She wondered why she hadn't been informed. After all, not only was she a member, she was also the one they'd asked to do all their legwork regarding the development.

"We had the meeting at the admiral's place early this afternoon, and Billy made it abundantly clear to everyone that you had no more knowledge of his being behind the development than anyone else had, and that we were being unfair for blaming you."

"I see," she said coolly. "And just like that, you all believed him?" *While none of you was willing to believe me?* She didn't say it, but Kevin, who wasn't stupid, caught her meaning.

He cleared his throat. "The man can be very . . . persuasive when he wants to be. But then, he always did have a silver tongue. And he, uh, he's made a substantial donation toward having the tennis courts resurfaced."

"How nice," she said dryly, and tactfully terminated the conversation a few moments later, her mind filled with angry and conflicting thoughts.

So Billy had bought back her neighbors' good will for her. The idea rankled her. Why couldn't they have continued to think well of her without his intervention? And when events of the next few days showed her that her neighbors meant to continue using her as a liaison between them and the developers, that's exactly how she felt: used.

She was dismayed to learn that because Billy had championed her, most of them believed she had some influence over him.

"You're the only one who can make him see reason, dear," said Mrs. Hamilton. "He must listen to someone! I got the impression he's still very much, well, shall we say, enamored of you? I realize, naturally, that you are engaged to that lovely doctor, and anyway, it would be most inappropriate if you and

Billy were to . . . you know. Think of how your grandparents would feel, considering that his mother was their housekeeper. But since he . . . likes you, I believe he'll listen to you. It's dreadfully unfair that he means to place the full width of the greenbelt to benefit *your* property—and his, of course. Don't think we aren't all aware of that."

Arlene sighed silently and gently reminded Mrs. Hamilton that the natural land configurations would provide the needed barrier.

Eventually, though, she conceded that Mrs. Hamilton did have a point, and hung up after reluctantly agreeing to talk to Billy. Mrs. Hamilton must have put the word around, because several more people called with their concerns regarding the lack of a buffer at the northern boundary of the new development.

"Could I see you for a few minutes this evening?" Arlene asked, phoning Billy after dinner.

His voice was low, teasing, and all too seductive. "Arlie, you can see me any time of the day or night. All you have to do is show up at my door." He chuckled and added, "But I don't recommend it tonight. There are seven little girls scrambling all over the motor home and leaving trails of potato chips and cola everywhere." He spoke loudly over the raucous music in the background. "How about my coming to your place?"

"Oh, right! The sleepover. I'd forgotten, though I don't know how I could have, I heard so much about it today. No, I won't bother you tonight. This will keep."

"You'd be doing me a favor, getting me out of this din," he said. "I thought it was only teenagers who had to have their music too loud."

"At the age of eight or nine they probably like to think they're almost teenagers," she said. She wondered how he'd like the dances at Marcy's school.

There, the noise was horrendous. She wore earplugs when she attended.

"I'll be over in half an hour."

"You don't need to. I can see you tomorrow. No, correction, Monday. I have to go to Seattle tomorrow." She had decided she would see her daughter this weekend regardless. She couldn't let Billy's presence and her probably unfounded fears keep her locked away from Marcy. Besides, she'd read enough detective stories that she was sure she could throw off a tail if she had to.

"Oh," he said. "I was about to say that tomorrow is out for me too. I'm driving Holly to the airport. She's going to spend a few days with Sherril. The show's taking a brief hiatus. But listen, why don't you come with us? After we drop her off, we could have lunch, talk, you could do what you need to do, and then we could meet up again, maybe even see a show and have dinner."

Arlene crushed down the wish that she could accept his invitation and said, "No thanks. I'll be busy all day and I'm spending the night with a friend. And I'll need my car."

She heard a note of hardness enter his tone. "All right. Let's make it this evening. Mavis can come over and ride herd on this mob, and I really do need a break."

She didn't argue further, and when she opened the door to Billy, the old familiar ache filled her chest.

"Hi," he said, not smiling, but lifting a hand to touch her face, the way he always did. Even though she knew how wrong it was for her to take so much pleasure in it, she didn't move away until his hand fell to his side. "You look pretty." His gaze lingered on her full breasts under the soft knit of her peach-colored sweater.

"Thanks." She turned and led the way into the

living room, feeling him right behind her. "Have a seat."

"Okay." He noticed the nervous twisting of her hands as she sat on the edge of a chair across from him. "What's wrong, Arlie?"

"Nothing, really," she said. "I'm a little concerned, is all."

"What about?" he asked, leaning toward her, his eyes intent on her face. "How can I help?"

"Why are you so adamant about not leaving any greenbelt at all on the north side of the development?" she said quickly, without preamble.

His eyes took on a lazy, half-shuttered look as he leaned back and stretched his legs out in front of him. He propped his elbows on the arms of his chair and rested his chin on his tented fingers. "Well, hell," he said. "And here I thought it was . . . personal." He shook his head slowly, his gaze never leaving her face. "Do you want to know because *you* want to know, or because they do? I mean, is this your concern, or someone else's?"

"*They* being the property owners to the north, of course?"

A dimple flashed briefly in his left cheek. "Of course."

"All right. They asked me to talk to you about it. They do have some legitimate concerns, you know."

"So they keep insisting. I've heard all this before, about a dozen times, from half a dozen different people. Why should it be different because you're asking me?"

"I don't know!" she flared. "Like I said, they asked me."

"And you agreed? After the way they treated you? After the name-calling and unfounded accusations?"

"They . . . couldn't help reacting that way," she defended her neighbors. "We Islanders have always stuck together. You didn't need to go to bat for me, Billy. They'd have seen eventually that they were wrong."

He grinned sourly. "You're welcome."

With an angry puff of breath she blew her hair off her forehead. "All right, all right. Thank you."

"Very graciously put. Your grandmother would be proud of you. Like you said, 'We Islanders have always stuck together.' In case you're forgetting, I'm legitimately an Islander now, Arlene. Of course I wanted to take your part when you were being treated unfairly."

"Billy, I don't need your sarcasm, and I'm sick to death of people dragging my grandparents and their opinions into every conversation! Why don't you stop tormenting those people and say that you'll leave a band of trees between the boat yard and the base of the hill?"

He grinned. "You mean that's all I have to do? Merely *say* that I'll do it, so they'll get off my back? And yours."

She thumped a fist on an arm of her chair. "No, dammit, saying you will won't be enough! You know as well as I do that the hill is sparsely treed, and that Mrs. Hamilton's gazebo is right up on top, where the view is best out over the Sound. If you cut down all the big trees behind her gazebo, she'll be looking right into your operation. And on the Rushes' property line, the hill's nothing more than a low, rocky bluff with no trees at all. They're going to get the noise and dust from your access road. Please, Billy, be a good neighbor even if it means leaving fewer trees on this side and more on that one."

"No."

"Dammit, you're carrying vengeance too far! Isn't it enough that you're going to have your boat yard and your housing development? Do you have to rub their noses in it as well by making them aware of it every day?"

"Why not?" He looked cocky and devilish and was clearly enjoying hearing her beg on behalf of the other Islanders. "The land is mine. I can do what I want with it." It infuriated her and she leapt to her feet, hands on hips, glaring at him."

"Billy, grow up! You're long past the bad-boy stage. Leave that kind of stuff in the past, where it belongs. You've showed them, you idiot! You have them—if not liking you, if not accepting you—at the very least aware of your power. Most of the Islanders are old, and they're scared. Mr. and Mrs. Rush have gone so far as to build a chain-link fence around the grounds adjacent to their house because they're worried about the 'riffraff' who'll be living on the Island not a mile from their home."

"I'm not changing my plans."

"Kevin Morrison is making ominous sounds regarding court cases," she warned him.

"Let him make any kind of sounds he wants." Billy shrugged negligently. "All that would do is slow me down. It wouldn't stop me."

"You're being a pain in the . . . dammit, you could compromise by moving the boat yard out of Anderson Bay and using Lockyer instead," she said, sitting down again, but still glaring.

He managed to hide his surprise. Arlene knew the shoreline of the Island as well as he did. She'd have seen why he'd chosen Anderson Bay, with its shallow-pitched beach and deep dropoff a very few feet from the low-tide mark. She was as aware as he was that Lockyer made an adequate second choice, and if he left Anderson Bay alone, the stand of forest could be saved.

"It's not a bad compromise, Billy," she said.

He gave her a hard look. Dammit, when had anyone on this island ever compromised to make *his* life easier?

"Sorry," he said, sounding totally unapologetic. "But the Council has approved our plans and the first equipment will be crossing the bridge Tuesday morning next week."

The bridge? Suddenly, Arlene smiled. Why hadn't she thought of it sooner? "No," she said quietly. "It won't."

Billy narrowed his gaze on her. He didn't like that smile. "Why not?"

"Because that bridge, and the land at both its ends, sits on Lambert property and, as the Lambert who owns it, I have the power to stop your moving anything over that bridge—your carcass included. Now, either you get reasonable pretty damned fast, Billy Culver, or your project lies dead in the water."

Billy sat up straight. "You wouldn't!"

"Watch me!"

"And what about the benefit to the community? What about the housing? The jobs? The park? New contracts for the mill? You'd see all that go down the tubes to spite me?"

"Why not? You're going out of your way to spite some people I care about. I'm not asking for something impossible, and you know it. A greenbelt, Billy. Move the project a mile this way into Lockyer Bay. There's plenty of room to do that. Give them their privacy, their solitude. Don't detract from their property values because some of them hurt your feelings when you were a child."

It had gone deeper than that, much deeper, and she knew it as well as he did. He got to his feet and loomed over her, fists clenched, eyes narrowed.

"I don't need your bridge, Arlene Lambert," he said in a low, angry growl. "I'll barge my equipment in if I have to."

Even as he said it, he knew it was impossible, or

at the very least, wildly impractical. That was one of the first things they'd investigated, for God's sake, and here he was, spouting off like the damn fool he was, saying things he had no business saying.

The cost of barging was prohibitive, and there was no loading site nearby. The engineers all agreed that even if the bridge had required upgrading and reinforcement in order to take the heavy equipment, it would have been cheaper than barging. That the bridge was sound had merely been a bonus to the company and . . . Oh, hell, he was going to lose the whole damned thing before it ever got off the ground! He'd come this far and it was all starting to fall apart!

What the hell was he going to tell his advisors and backers, people who were not only his friends, but who believed in him enough to invest in every project he ran? They were going to go absolutely snakey when he told them this little bit of news!

He remembered Glenn advising him not to get soft in the head over a woman, not to get hard in the . . . And here, he'd done both.

With a gusty sigh he slumped back down in the chair. Dammit, it was time to do some swift backtracking.

"All right, all right," he said. "I don't want to let you down, and I know the other Islanders rely on you. So, okay. I'll think about a stand of trees at the base of the hill. Half a mile deep, though. Not a mile. We still need room to swing that road through there. And there's a condition."

She looked at him warily. He'd given in too easily. She'd anticipated a long, involved battle over this matter. "What condition?"

He smiled, leaned forward and spoke very, very softly. "Nothing terrible, Arlie. Only that you marry me."

She looked at him, not sure she'd heard those words. She looked into the depths of his blue eyes and saw that he was not joking, that he had meant what he said, solemnly and sincerely. After all these years she was hearing what she'd once yearned to hear. Now she was forced to say no, no matter what her heart urged her to do.

That heart of hers . . . It hammered hard in her chest. She tried to speak and could not. She tried to swallow and could not. She tried to stand and could not. Her mind screamed at her to get up and run, to leave Billy and his blue, tempting eyes, his soft, tempting question, his beckoning, tempting hand, far behind.

"Arlie? Have you gone into shock? I don't know why, sweetheart. I told you two weeks ago that I was falling in love with you again. Didn't you believe me?"

From a long distance she heard him speak, and nodded her head. She'd believed him. Also from that same remote place she noticed that his hand, extended toward her, was trembling visibly.

"Then say something. Say yes."

She shook her head and forced herself up by pushing on the arms of her chair with icy hands and leaden arms.

"Oh, God," she whispered, speaking more to herself than to him. "This is . . . the most terrible moment of my life."

She moved away from where he was sitting, and his gaze followed her, almost clung to her. He had a strange expression on his face, one she had never seen before, which was odd, because she thought she knew him as well as she knew herself. But right now, he was alien, a little frightening, and utterly magnetizing.

"You know, Arlie, you're the first woman I've ever asked to marry me. I didn't expect it to be like this. I didn't expect you to look and act as if I'm asking you to do something unnatural and repugnant."

She blinked. In a way, that was what he was doing. She focused, though, on something else. "The first? Sherril—"

"Asked me," he said with a grin that didn't quite make it to his eyes. "So will you? It's the only way you'll get what you want for your friends."

The horror-stricken expression on her face deepened. "I . . . can't." Her voice was a pained whisper.

He raised his brows. "Can't?" He laughed softly, praying it was all a strange, feminine kind of joke, one he didn't understand but which would be explained to him if he kept on treating it lightly. "Don't you go throwing Sam in my face, Arlie."

"I . . . it's not Sam. There's someone else. You've known that. In . . . Seattle. What do you think I do when I go away for weekends? Go bowling?"

Billy saw the lie in her wounded gray eyes, along with the fear and the need and a hundred other conflicting emotions. He wanted to go to her and comfort her, show her how it could be and *should* be, even after all these years apart.

He knew it would be possible to overcome her objections with sex. He knew he could seduce her, make her say yes by the sheer power of his physical presence. And he wanted to, wanted it so bad he could taste it.

So why didn't he? What kept him frozen in his chair, not going to her, not touching her? Where had all the damned scruples come from all of a sudden? He didn't know, but they were there, and he had to let them lead him. He had to believe that soon, very soon, she would admit on her own that her need for him was as great as his for her.

She had to stop telling him no.

She had to stop these infernal lies!

"Fine, then. We'll both be in Seattle tomorrow. Introduce me to your . . . friend. Just as proof. Then, maybe, I'll withdraw my condition. And my proposal."

"Why should I need to prove anything to you? Why don't you simply believe me?"

He lost patience, which had never been one of his virtues anyway. Hell, he'd never had any virtue he didn't lose easily. "I don't believe you because I know you're lying," he said, getting up and moving slowly toward her.

Arlene stared up at him. She was mesmerized by the taut look of determination on his face as he came closer and spoke in a quiet, measured tone. "You can't prove to me that you're involved with another man because there's nothing to prove."

"I don't have to prove a damn thing to you! My life has nothing to do with you!"

He clamped his hands over her shoulders, unable to keep them off her one minute longer. "It has everything to do with me. You're still single at thirty-four because you can't find anybody to compare with me!"

Arlene lifted her hands and smashed his arms outward with her wrists, knocking him away. "Leave me alone!" she shouted, jamming her fists into her hair as she reeled away from him. "Just get out of my house, out of my life. Go back to Ellen! She's your kind and you're her kind. The two of you fit!"

"Ellen!" he said scathingly, trapping Arlene against the window seat. "Hell, I want her about as much as you want Sam."

"Oh, yeah? So why have you been dating her?"

"To make you jealous!" he roared, grabbing her and slamming her against his chest. "Did it work?"

"Yes!" she shrieked. "Damn you, yes! I hate you, Billy Culver! I hate you like the poison you are!"

"No you don't! You want me! You want me so bad you're shaking, just like I'm shaking because if I don't have you again, if I don't bury myself inside you and make love to you until you melt with passion, I'm going to go insane! Arlene, please, give in to it! Give in to me! Tell me you want me!"

"I do, I do." She wept, collapsing against him. "Oh, God, Billy, I don't know what to do!"

"Sweetheart." He gentled his hold on her, lifting her ravaged face to his and kissing her tenderly. "What to do is marry me."

Her sobs were loud and tearing and anguished in the quiet of the big house. "I can't," she moaned, rolling her head on his chest. "I can't! It's what I want more than I've ever wanted anything in my life, but it's the one thing I can never, ever do!"

"Arlene, why?"

"Because I have a daughter, Billy. A beautiful, wonderful child who is the light of my life. But she's deaf and blind and has been since birth."

ELEVEN

▼

Hurt slammed into Billy. He shuddered with it, setting her back from him and staring into her face as if she were a stranger.

Oh, hell, he'd known on an intellectual level that Arlene was probably sleeping with Sam. He'd known on the same level that she'd probably slept with other men. But his heart hadn't known it. And now a child? She'd had a baby? She'd carried some guy's child inside her?

No! Something inside him bellowed. For the first time, he was forced to acknowledge that Arlene had lain with some other man, opened her legs to him and let him pump his seed into her to make a baby! The thought created another picture: Arlene, a daffodil dress, green grass. The sensation returned of claiming her virginity with his hard thrusts and he cried out hoarsely.

No! He denied it again as the truth smashed into him. If she had a baby, that baby was his! His and Arlene's! She had kept her child a secret from him because he was its father. What had she said all those weeks ago? She hadn't tried to find him, hadn't told him about the cottage because she didn't want him to come back! And why hadn't she? Because she had a child she was hiding from him. It didn't make any kind of sense at all.

He groaned, felt his knees cave in and collapsed onto the window seat, dragging her down with him onto his lap. He buried his face against her shoulder while he struggled with the intense desire to strangle her if she'd kept more than a damned cottage from him.

Slowly, so slowly, he brought himself under control and started thinking about what she had said. Deaf? Blind? Since birth? And for that reason she thought she couldn't marry him? Was that the reason she hadn't told him?

What the hell did she think he wanted, perfection? If she was afraid to have more kids, so what? They had two. That would be enough!

When he could, he lifted his head and looked at her long and hard.

"Say something," she whispered. "Don't just look at me like that. As if you hate me."

"I do. I think I hate you more at this moment than I have ever hated anyone in my entire life." His voice shook. His eyes were indigo. "But I also love you more. Do you honestly think that your daughter's problems would make me want you less, would have any bearing on whether you and I should marry? Make a home together for her and Holly? My God, Arlene! Do you really think I'm that low?"

"No. No, it's not that."

"Then what? Why? She's mine, isn't she, Arlie? For once in your life, tell me the truth. Is that child mine?"

Slowly, she nodded.

He placed his forehead against hers for several seconds, breathing hard, his hands trembling on her upper arms. "Mine. All this time. My child. My first born. And you hid her from me. Damn, Arlie, it hurts! But it doesn't make me want you less." He lifted his head and looked at her. "It doesn't make me love you less. I want you and our daughter, and me and my daughter! We'll be a family, love. Together."

He smiled tautly, his blue eyes alight now, his face regaining color. "Together," he repeated. "Won't we? Arlie?"

"No . . ." Staring at him, she shook her head wildly. "Billy, you have to listen. Please . . ."

But he wanted answers, not arguments. "Why isn't she with you?" he asked excitedly. "God, she must be close to seventeen! What's her name. What does she look like? When can I meet her? How come nobody in Oakmount has mentioned her to me? Everybody talks about you all the time, about how wonderful you are. You'd think raising a handicapped daughter all alone would be something else for them to boast about on your behalf!"

Arlene drew in a deep, unsteady breath. "Billy, this just gets harder and harder."

"Then take it one step at a time, sweetheart. What's her name?"

"Marcy."

"Marcy. Marcy Lambert." He frowned. "Her name is Lambert? Or did you give her my name?"

"No," she said. "She bears my name."

"It doesn't matter. We can have it changed to what it should be, or I'll adopt her. Marcy Culver. How does that sound? God, won't Holly be ecstatic? She's always wanted a sister. Have you told her about Marcy?"

"No. Billy, for heaven's sake, be quiet!" She took his face in her hands. "Listen to me. You can't adopt her. You and I can't get married. We won't create a family. Get that through your head right now. It is not going to happen. There are . . . reasons."

He moved her off his lap because the warmth of her bottom was making him hard, and even he could see this was not the time for that. He half turned, facing her, swinging one leg onto the window seat to block her into the corner so she couldn't escape if she wanted to.

"Okay," he said. "Give me those reasons of yours."

Arlene knew by his tone that he was discounting her reasons without ever hearing them. "Start at the beginning." He grimaced. "No, don't. I know the beginning as well as you do. Start with when you knew you were pregnant. Why didn't you try to find me?"

She didn't answer, merely looking down at her hands for a moment, then up at him again.

"Oh, God," she whispered, "will you accept that what you want is impossible? I don't care about the trees or the development or my neighbors. I don't care about anything. I just don't want to talk about this anymore."

"Arlene, the damned boat yard can go anywhere you say! Hell, I'll even cancel my plans for putting it here, buy land on the other side of the inlet and put it over there! But you've got to tell me about our daughter and why you're so convinced that you and I can't be together! Dammit, I love you. And you aren't getting away with lying to me any longer!" He tilted her face up with an ungentle hand. "Understand?"

She nodded almost resignedly.

"Then talk, dammit! Talk."

Drawing in a deep breath, she began.

"When I told my grandmother I was pregnant, she was very angry, very upset with me. Dad was away, of course, so Grandma dealt with the situation herself, in her own way. Oh, she told him, but only after she'd made all the arrangements." Arlene made a sad little face. "That's when she told me what was going to happen. She sent me to an unwed mother's home in Connecticut so no one would ever know. You see, she felt I had shamed the family, that I had disgraced not only myself, but her. I was supposed to put the baby up for adoption, then come back here for college. Where she could keep an eye on me." Her voice trembled as she added, "But when Marcy was born, I knew I couldn't. Nothing on earth would have made me give her up."

"Because she was blind and deaf?" he asked gently, leaning forward, smoothing her hair back behind her left ear.

His touch was too tender, too tempting. Arlene slid farther back into the corner of the window seat, picked up a cushion, and cuddled it against her abdomen.

"No," she said. "Because I adored her. I didn't suspect her blindness for a month or more, and even when I did, I wasn't sure what was wrong, only that there was . . . something. The doctors kept saying that some children learn to focus a little later than others, that I was a nervous new mom. But I knew. Something in me knew she had some very serious problems. For one thing, she never smiled. And she rolled her head from side to side incessantly as if . . . searching for something.

"I went to doctor after doctor, and finally, when she was six months old, they did some extensive tests and we learned she had virtually no sight in her left eye and only ten percent in her right. That meant she could see light and shadow, but nothing more."

Arlene's chin wobbled for a second, and she blinked hard. "She lost that little bit of sight when she was three."

Billy clenched his teeth and his fists in order not to touch her. He wanted to hold her, wanted this never to have happened, wanted to have been there

with her to share the fear and the pain and the feeling of helplessness she must have gone through all
alone. All alone? Why had she had to be all alone?
It was monstrous! If he had known, somehow, he'd
have found a way to help her.

"Your grandmother wasn't rich anymore. I know
that," he said. "But she still had friends, connec-
tions! Why didn't you find me?"

"Billy . . . she wouldn't have helped me look for
you. You know she wouldn't! Anyway, I never told
her who Marcy's father was, but of course she
suspected."

"All right. Yes. Go on."

She sat there, staring at nothing. "Arlie? Tell me
about Marcy. The . . . deafness? When did you learn
about that?"

She wrapped her arms tighter around the cushion.
"That was diagnosed at the same time," she said,
then sat silently, looking, he thought, back into a
grim and unhappy past.

"What did you do?" he prompted finally to get
her going again. Until they got this sorted out, they
couldn't even begin to work on whatever she felt
was holding him and her apart. "Did your grandmother let you come home then? Did she help?"

Arlene shook her head. "I didn't tell her. I didn't
even tell her I hadn't given Marcy up. We weren't
in touch very often. But I had some debentures my
grandfather had bought in my name and that I could
cash in because I was over eighteen. That was
enough for me to go to college as well as pay for
Marcy's care and schooling."

"You had to put her in an institution?"

Her gaze flew to his face at his troubled tone.
"No. At least, not then. And Billy, there are institutions and . . . institutions. But at that time Marcy
and I lived with a wonderful woman who was a
retired teacher of deaf children. One of the nurses I

met during Marcy's testing and evaluation sessions put me in touch with her. I could never have done it without Opal. Together we taught Marcy to smile and laugh and play and—"

"To smile?" he interrupted.

"Babies smile at people because people smile at babies. She'd never seen anybody smile, so how could she know to do it? It was the same with laughter, with play. She had to be taught. She even had to be taught to crawl and walk."

"Taught to *crawl*?" He remembered that there had been no stopping Holly once she'd decided she wanted to crawl.

"Yes. Without sight or hearing, she had no incentive to move from place to place. In fact, she was scared to. So Opal and I taught her everything—smiling, crawling, walking, even holding her head at the proper angle. Without that we could never have gotten her into a school. Everyone insisted she was stupid. But she wasn't. She isn't. She's . . . wonderful, Billy."

The deep frustration Arlene had experienced came through, and Billy gritted his teeth in empathy. God, what a terrible time it had been for her! And she'd been alone! That in itself made him angrier than he knew he had a right to be. It was his fault. He had used her and left her. Left her alone and pregnant.

"Some experts called her autistic, too, as well as retarded, but for whatever reason, uneducable." Now she smiled, triumph clear in her expression. "Opal and I—and Marcy—showed them different."

"How?"

"By teaching Marcy. By showing them all that she could learn, and wanted to learn, that she was as smart as any kid who could see and hear. Lacking what are known as 'distance senses,' sight and hearing, she had no inclination to explore her world.

Her world consisted of what was within her random reach. We had to make her want to discover what was beyond her reach by letting her know that there were things out there and that there were rewards in seeking them. It was a twenty-four-hour-a-day, seven-day-a-week proposition, and if Opal hadn't insisted, I wouldn't have found the courage to leave Marcy with her and go to school myself. By the time I got my degree, and a job teaching special-needs groups, Marcy was ready for residential school."

His brows drew together. "Aren't blind and deaf kids classed as special needs? Couldn't you teach Marcy yourself? Have her with you here?"

"Marcy's not with me because she needs to be in a residential school where she can get the best education possible. Like I said, her learning process needs to be controlled and managed all day, every day, three hundred and sixty-five days a year. Of course, we're together for vacations and holidays, but she loves being at school. She plans to become a teacher herself. And as for my teaching her, you know what you said about you and Holly. The same thing applies to us. We both got too frustrated and angry with each other when things didn't go quite right."

"So you put her in school." He shook his head slowly. "I remember when Holly started, how it scared me to send my baby out every morning to be cared for by strangers. And your child didn't even come home at night. It must have been pretty terrible."

"It wasn't easy. For either of us. For the first few weeks I moved right into the school with her until she was used to being there and having other people care for her. They were wonderful, the staff in that school."

"Was that in Connecticut?" Her nod elicited a frown. "She's not still there, is she?"

"No. She's in a private school in Seattle." She bit her lip. "She's the one I go to see most weekends."

His smile was one of total relief. "Of course. How long ago did you come back to Washington?"

"My grandmother got quite sick about a year before she died and begged me to come home. I told her about Marcy, and she was sorry that I'd gone through all that alone, when she could have helped me carry the load."

"As she damned well should have been! How could someone who loved you have been so unforgiving? Did she think you'd gotten pregnant all by yourself? That you'd done it because you were promiscuous? Dammit, she knew you! She'd raised you. She must have been able to figure out that it's usually the innocent girls who get caught, not the ones who make a habit of screwing around."

"Billy, she was of a different generation. She felt I had shamed her. She forgave me in the end, and I forgave her, too, so we were able to be happy together for her last year. I've always been glad of that."

"And Marcy? Did she learn to love your daughter?"

Arlene shifted her gaze uncomfortably. "She saw her only a couple of times."

"Why?" he demanded indignantly. "The *shame* thing? She couldn't bring herself to see an illegitimate child?"

"She wasn't well enough to travel," Arlene retorted angrily.

He eyed her suspiciously. "You didn't bring Marcy here?"

Again she evaded his gaze. "I, well, no."

Suddenly, it all made sense, why no one had mentioned Marcy to him. "You still don't, do you?" he accused. "You never have."

She shook her head and sighed, meeting his eyes this time. "No. No, Marcy's never been here. Only a few people know about her. Sam does, of course, and Miss Quail." She gave him a half-smile. "Miss Quail adores her because she looks just like you."

"She does?" he said, his eyes lighting up for a moment before he remembered. "So that explains why nobody told me about Marcy! Who else knows?"

"My father, of course. A few of my personal friends."

Now he caught on completely. "But none of the Islanders, right? You're still protecting your grandmother, aren't you? The precious family name. My God, Arlie, she's dead! What do you care now about her so-called 'shame'? About the good Lambert name? Even if she weren't dead, she'd have no right to keep you from acknowledging your own child and bringing her home with you!"

What could she say? He was right in a way. While her grandmother lived, she hadn't wanted her "disgraceful" deed to embarrass the old lady. Then, after Letitia died, and Arlene had found those telltale letters, she knew she could never let anyone see Marcy for fear that Billy would someday, some way, learn of her existence.

She sighed again. Yet for all her careful hiding of the facts, for all her treating her daughter as a secret, though never one she was personally ashamed of, Billy was going to have to know. She had no more choices left. He had to be told because he wasn't going to take no for an answer unless he knew the truth.

She quailed at the thought. It was going to be difficult to find the right words. How she hated to hurt him with the knowledge of his mother's actions with Arlene's adulterous grandfather. He might be broadminded when it came to himself and others, but a man's mother was . . . almost sacred.

"After Grandma died," she went on, "I thought about selling this place, but I couldn't bring myself to do it. It was Marcy's heritage as much as mine. And since I needed an income, I opened my school and day care."

"Couldn't you get a job teaching in Marcy's school? Not teaching her, but others? Or maybe at a different school nearby?"

She shook her head. "I guess I could have, but this way my living expenses are at a minimum and most of what I earn can go to keeping Marcy in her school."

Billy nodded, but she could see his mind was elsewhere. "What caused those defects anyway?" he asked. "Did you have rubella?"

She closed her eyes. If only it had been that simple. "No."

"Then what? Why is Marcy the way she is?"

She licked her lips, bit the lower one, and looked down at her hands. "I'm not certain. But I think it's probably because . . . because you and I are . . . blood relatives."

He started, reared back from her, and got to his feet. "What?" He paced away, whirled, and stared at her. "Arlie, that's . . . *insane!*" he exploded, driving one fist into the opposing palm, his eyes wild, his face white.

"Billy." She stood. Her legs wobbled. She walked toward him. "Let me show you some letters I found a long time ago."

He scowled. What was going on here? Arlie's face was white again, her hands shaking. Her breath came in jagged little puffs as she went first to the desk for a key, then to a cupboard, where she crouched, unlocked a low drawer, and took out a small box. Dammit, she *believed* what she'd told him. And had letters to prove it? Impossible!

"Here," she said, opening it on the dining table under the overhead fixture, which she turned up to its brightest setting. "These confirm it, Billy."

He opened the first one, recognized with a pang his mother's hand, and began to read the words meant never to be seen except by the man she loved, by her . . . lover.

A cruel memory of the judge and his mother flashed in his brain—bodies heaving, white buttocks, legs looped over . . . His heart denied it even while his gut reacted and he gagged. He twisted away from Arlene's compassionate gaze.

"No!" he shouted against the horror that encompassed him, against the conviction he'd seen in her solemn gaze. "No!" he shouted again. Then, in an agony of denial, he reeled away from her and pounded a fist into the wall, cracking the antique paneling in two places. "Goddamn it, Arlene! It's a lie! It can't be true! I won't let it be true! For the love of God, tell me it isn't true!" He spun, facing her.

She knew how hard it had been for her to face the truth. For him, it must be doubly, triply hard. She wept softly, his anguish her own. "Yes. It's true. Oh, Billy. I'm so sorry! I never wanted you to know. If I could have kept it from you, I would have, but you wouldn't leave me alone, you wouldn't stop pushing! I love you. You know that. But we can't marry each other, ever, and now you know why. My grandfather . . . Your mother . . . They never *meant* to hurt anyone, I'm sure, but Billy . . . Oh God, please, wait!"

He stared at her from tortured eyes set deep into a colorless face then staggered away, out the door, leaving it swinging open behind him in the wind.

TWELVE

A long time later Arlene realized that her shivering might have something to do with rapidly dropping temperature in the house. With aching bones she went to the door and closed it. Then, too weary even to climb the stairs to bed, she curled on the sofa under a blanket and slid into sleep, hiding there, wishing she could remain in its safety forever. But at dawn she was jarred awake by the sound of hammering on her door.

"Take me to her," said Billy, slumping against the doorframe. "Take me to my daughter. It's time we met."

Arlene stood back and let him in. She met his obdurate, determined gaze, and nodded. Argument would be futile. "What time is Holly's plane?"

"Nine-thirty. I want to leave in an hour. Can you be ready?"

She nodded again, her throat suddenly too tight to talk. He looked like hell. He looked like she felt.

As if reading her expression, he said, "I went to Tulane's last night. For the first time in ten years, I ordered a drink."

"No," she whispered. *She* had done that to him!

"I didn't drink it. I sat and looked into it for half an hour. Then I got up and left."

"Billy . . ."

"I ran. Ran and walked. Ran and walked. Until it

179

was all I could do to make it back to my car." He smiled tautly. "But I didn't take that drink."

"Oh, God. I'm so sorry for what I'm doing to you."

"I'm sorry for what I *did* to you." He plucked at the sleeve of her sweater, glanced at her creased pants. "You didn't go to bed?"

"I fell asleep on the sofa."

"I didn't sleep at all."

"Then I'll drive to the airport."

"The hell you will. I drive."

"Sorry. I have a child dependent on me, and I don't intend to raise her from a wheelchair because I took a ride with a man suffering from sleep deprivation."

"Oh, hell," he said, shoving a shaking hand into his thick hair. "Suit yourself. But we take my car. Meet us at the cottage when you're ready." He turned to leave.

"Does Holly know?"

Arlene's question stopped him. He gave her a long look. "No. I figured it was your story to tell."

"Thank you."

"You're welcome. Arlene?"

"Yes?"

"Marcy is no longer solely dependent on you. I'll make the same kind of provisions for her in my will as I have for Holly. And start taking over her school expenses."

Her eyes flared. "No!"

His were narrow slits. "Yes." It was said very, very softly, and Arlene did not argue further at the moment.

"I never wanted you to know about your grandfather and my mother," Billy said when they were back in the car after seeing Holly onto her plane. He had taken the wheel and, since he'd slept most of the way to SeaTac, Arlene didn't object.

"What do you mean? I had no idea you knew until I told you last night. That was part of why I didn't bring Marcy home. She looks so much like you that anybody would know you were her father. And I was pretty sure of your reaction if you ever knew about her and made the connection. I didn't want you ever to have to know. Any of it."

"I knew about their affair years ago. I walked in on them when I was a teenager. They never knew I was there."

She reached over and put her hand on the back of his, smoothing her fingertips across knuckles made white by his tight grip on the steering wheel. "That must have been a terrible time for you."

Turning his hand over, he captured hers and held it against his leg. "And for you, when you found out, but I don't suppose you went out and got drunk the way I did. Why in the world did she tell you, I wonder," he said musingly. "Surely it was something she'd rather have kept to herself."

"Who?" asked Arlene. "You lost me somewhere." She pulled her hand away from his. Touching him felt too . . . right, and feeling like that was all wrong.

He cut a glance her way. "Your grandmother, of course."

"My *grandmother*?" She sucked in a harsh breath and turned her pained gaze on him. "Oh, God, do you think she knew, Billy? I don't want to believe that! That was one thing I've always been able to comfort myself with—that she went to her death believing Grandpa had loved her exclusively all those years, been a faithful and loving husband!"

The car jerked alarmingly before Billy headed it straight again. "Are you saying she didn't tell you?" he demanded.

"No, she didn't tell me! Even if she knew, it wouldn't have been something she'd tell me! Right up to the time she died, Grandma saw me as a little girl."

"Then how the hell did you find out?"

"When Grandma died and I learned the cottage was yours, I went over there because I'd seen some bundles of letters when I first packed up your mom's things. The ones I showed you last night, as it turned out. I thought they might be from some relatives or friends of hers I could contact for information about where you'd gone." She sighed. "Well, to shorten it, I started reading the letters and soon discovered what they were all about. They told their own story. Grandpa and your mom had been lovers for years before he brought the two of you here to live, and suddenly, Marcy's birth defects started to make a sick kind of sense. I had to ask myself, what if Billy is my grandfather's son? My dad's half-brother? My uncle?"

She half turned in the seat and looked at him imploringly. "What if you and I share some kind of wonky gene, and in our producing Marcy, it was doubled? That was why, when I could have contacted you and told you about the cottage, I didn't."

He stared at her. "My God!" he said, and when she gasped in alarm at the car's dangerous swerve, he wrenched it back into the right lane.

"So. You see it, too, don't you? Why we can never take the chance of marrying one another. Because there is no way to know for certain, Billy, that we aren't related by blood."

He flipped on the turn signal, changed lanes rapidly, and zipped down an exit ramp, finally pulling over on a grassy verge. He shut off the engine and turned to stare at her. "My . . . God," he said again, slowly. "A *suspicion*? All you have is a suspicion, Arlie? On that you're willing to screw up our lives?

I thought you *knew* I was your illegitimate uncle! I thought your grandmother had *told* you. That the old man had confessed it to her! But you honestly don't know beyond a suspicion?"

"I know enough! I know they had an affair, your mother and my grandfather! An affair that started way back before he even became a judge. Maybe even before you were born. You saw those letters, the dates on them, and read the references to things said and done 'years ago.' How many years ago? That's what I had to ask myself. And I know he brought you both to the Island to live! I also know that my daughter has genetic defects that defy any other explanation! Dammit, I was a young, healthy woman in my prime! There was no reason for me to produce a child with multiple handicaps. Until I learned about Grandpa and Jenny, that is. Then I could see that there was a damn good reason!

"This is more than a guess, Billy. This is a reasoned supposition, a terrible burden that I've lived with daily for eleven long years, along with the grinding, ugly guilt that came with it. It's something that came damned close to putting me in the booby-hatch! If it hadn't been for some really good counseling from several different practitioners, I'd never have learned to deal with the ramifications of what I'd done."

"What *you'd* done?" he roared. "What, exactly, did *you* do that caused such terrible, ugly grinding guilt?"

"I conceived a child by my uncle!" she yelled back at him.

"Like hell you did!" He grabbed her upper arms and dragged her halfway across the console toward him, his eyes glittering with rage. "You conceived a child by the man you loved and who loved you and who had a right to know a daughter existed a hell of a lot sooner than her seventeenth year! Who the hell were you to keep that from me? By what God-given right did you decide for me . . . for *me*, Arlene, that I should be kept in the dark about my own firstborn child?"

"Being that child's mother gave me all the rights I needed! I wanted to protect Marcy from you, too. I knew from the very beginning that you'd react this way, that you'd want to see her, try to take her from me if that was the only way you could be with her and that you'd fight everyone on earth to keep her."

"Goddamn right!" he said, shaking her, his eyes blazing with fury. "Even you, Arlene Lambert! Especially you! You better believe I'll fight!"

"You go right ahead! You haven't got a hope in hell of taking her now!"

He gave her another shake. "Watch me, Arlie! I'll fight to keep her as hard as I'll fight to keep you!"

"You can't have me! Dammit, Billy, let me go!"

"Not in a million years, lady! You are my woman, not my niece!" he said scathingly. "You are the mother of one of my children, and you and I are going to quit messing around and wasting time! Dammit, Arlene, we belong together! We always have! We never should have let your family keep us apart!"

"Billy! For the love of God, don't you understand even now why they did?"

"No, dammit! No! I don't buy your theory, Arlene! I never will!"

"You have to, because it's the only one that makes any sense!"

"Not to me it doesn't. To me, the only thing that makes sense is this." Hands gripping her upper arms, he dragged her close and bent her head back in a deep and ferociously hungry kiss.

"Stop it! You're hurting me!" Arlene struggled against him, then hauled off and cuffed him across the left ear.

Billy flung open the car door and shot out of his seat. He leaned on the hood with both hands, his arms stiff, his head hanging down between them. He was panting. Moments later he came back and slumped against the side of the car, his eyes closed, his breathing still ragged. Arlene got out and went to his side. He sighed. "Sorry."

"Me too."

"Where do we go from here?"

"Literally?"

He hesitated, looking down at her, unhappiness surrounding him like a dark cloud. "Yeah. I guess so. Where is Marcy's school?"

"Get back onto 1-5," she said. "I'll direct you from there."

"Skiing?" Billy was aghast when they left the school. "They let her go skiing? How can she do that? She can't see. She can't hear! Dammit, she could get seriously hurt! Arlene, it's criminal to let a kid like Marcy take those risks."

"It would be more criminal to keep her locked up in a padded cell for safekeeping," she retorted, slamming the car door behind her. Billy glowered at her for a few minutes before striding around and getting behind the wheel. He was more than a little upset. He'd geared himself up to meet Marcy, only to discover upon arrival at the school that she was out on some cockamamy ski expedition, for God's sake! The whole idea defied common sense.

"How can you stand it?" he asked, his arms stiff, his fingers clenched around the wheel as if to strangle it. "I haven't even met her and I'm terrified for her."

"I got used to it," she said more gently. "I was scared for her, too, at first. When she learned to walk, when she learned to go up and down stairs, when she wanted to learn to ice skate as well as roller skate, I had nightmares. I've been scared for her so many times. I guess I've learned to hide it from myself as much as possible because I've had to hide it from her. I couldn't live my life being afraid all the time, Billy, or let her live that way either."

"No. I guess not." He was silent for several moments, staring straight ahead. Then, with one finger, he drew a line down the sleeve of her tan suede blazer, flicked at the fabric of her stylish dark-green slacks, and glanced at her high-heeled suede boots. "We're not exactly dressed for Mount Baker." He was wearing a slightly heavier jacket with dress slacks and loafers. "Are you sure you want to do this?"

She smiled. "Do you think you could contain your impatience until she gets back late tomorrow afternoon if we don't?"

After a moment he shook his head and started the car, pulling out onto the street. "A quick run up there, then. You introduce us and we visit for a while, then we head back."

"Sounds good to me. I'd hate to keep her off the slopes for too long. Skiing's one of her favorite sports. But first I should call my friend Irene and beg a bed for the night, in case she's out when we get back. I didn't tell her in advance that I'd be down here this weekend. I meant to do it from the airport, but I forgot. Pull into the next service station, okay, so I can call?

"Irene's got a houseful this weekend," Arlene said a few minutes later, getting back into the car. "But this time of year there won't be any problem getting into a hotel. Maybe we should both book rooms before we go up the mountain."

"We don't need to book rooms. I never planned on going back tonight either. I've got a suite reserved at the Bayshore because Mavis was coming with me to do some shopping but her throat was sore this morning—probably from having to yell over all that loud rock music. We could have dinner together and maybe do a little dancing or whatever and enjoy our unexpected evening in the city."

He spoke rapidly, not looking at her, but straight ahead out the windshield. "You wouldn't mind sharing a suite with me, would you? If it's a problem, we could get a room for you on another floor or even in a different hotel. But it seems a shame to let Mavis's room go to waste, and there's a lock on the door so you wouldn't have to worry, and I'm talking too much because I'm scared spitless about what you're going to tell Marcy about me and that you'll turn down my offer of the room because you don't trust me and why don't you tell me to shut up?" he ended, almost pleading with her.

"Billy," she said obligingly, "shut up." They shared a warm smile for a moment until the atmosphere between them began to heat and the smiles faded. They looked quickly away from each other, both thinking thoughts best left unspoken.

Thoughts of meeting Marcy weren't the only ones in his mind. Or hers. But they'd do for a distraction right now.

"You don't have to worry about being shocked or upset when I introduce you," she said. "Marcy knows what her father's name is. She knows, too, that you're in the neighborhood, so to speak. I told her a couple of weeks ago that you were back in Oakmount. She doesn't know, of course, that she'll be meeting you today. She's always known that might never happen."

"How much have you told her? I mean, about your theory?"

She let that pass. She believed it was far more than mere "theory," but it was pointless to argue the same ground over and over. She wished it weren't so easy for a part of her to listen to his words, to wonder if perhaps he wasn't related to her. She didn't dare think thoughts like that too often; they weakened her.

"I told her only that you and I were too young to marry and my family disapproved of you very much even though I loved you a lot."

"And now? Now that I'm back, doesn't she want to meet me?"

"Yes. I told her it might be . . . difficult."

"Difficult? How?"

"You won't be able to communicate with her very much at first," she said. "It'll be awkward for you. I'm sorry. I wish it could be different."

"Me too, babe. I wish a lot of things had been different. But from here on out they will be. Marcy has two parents now, regardless of what happens with you and me. I will learn to talk to her, and to understand what she's saying. I will be her father in every way."

Arlene let out a shaky breath and turned her head away, looking out at the pleasant green landscape sliding by. She yawned, then moments later jerked upright when she became aware that her head was nodding.

"Go to sleep, Arlie." Billy reached into the back-seat and grabbed the cushion Holly had brought. He handed it to her and she stuffed it between herself and the window and rested her head on it grate-fully. His hand was gentle as he massaged her neck, warm as he slipped it under her hair, then inside the collar of her jacket, strong as she let herself lean into it . . . for only a moment or two.

"I'll wake you when we get there," he promised, and she sighed, then slept.

Billy Culver, tough guy, sat on the edge of a hard bench because he didn't dare stand up for fear his knees would give way. His eyes stung with tears he refused to shed, his nose burned, and his throat ached as he looked into the face of his older daughter for the first time.

After their arrival, he and Arlene had stood in the nearly deserted glass-walled observation lounge, hand in hand for mutual support, while Marcy's sighted guide came whizzing down the hill with her, touching her arms alternately with ski poles, indicating turns, dips and hazards as they skimmed across the moist spring snow. Billy was glad to see that the two skiers were attached loosely by a rope, so that if an immediate stop were necessary, the line could be tugged taut.

"I'll go and get her before she gets on the chair lift again," Arlene had said, squeezing his hand before she left, and then he had sat near the big plate-glass windows, feeling the heat of the sun, the hardness of the seat, and panic rippling through his veins.

"Wait here," Arlie had added, giving him a concerned look. "We'll be fairly private here for a while until the lunch crowd comes in."

And, now she was back again, arm in arm with a dainty, beautiful young woman—Marcy, his daughter. She was suntanned, slightly burned, had freckles across the bridge of her small nose. Her dark curly hair spilled from beneath a red wool cap which she tugged off before shedding her thick gloves and bending to unsnap the buckles of her ski boots. She was a petite girl, slightly built, with delicate features, and fine brows shaped like wings. He'd seen twelve-year-olds bigger than Marcy, but she was all female, with gentle curves like Arlie's, and she had the same habit his mother had had of cocking her head to one side when she was asking a question.

"Who did you bring to meet me, Mom?" Marcy signed.

As she'd promised Billy earlier that she would, Arlene repeated the words Marcy's swift gestures conveyed to her, and spoke aloud each thing she told the girl.

"Someone special." As she spoke, Arlene's fingers made small, quick movements inside Marcy's cupped hands. "Someone who loves you very much, but who doesn't know how to talk to you yet. He plans to learn, though, so I want you to help him all you can. His name is . . ." And now Arlene's motions slowed slightly as her fingers formed individual letters. "Billy Culver."

Marcy's face went still and stiff. A small frown appeared between her flyaway brows. She grabbed Arlene's hand and moved her fingers inside it. "Daddy?"

"Yes. Your father. Will you say hello to him?"

Marcy nodded. Arlene reached for Billy's hand and curved Marcy's around it.

Her hand was cool and small on his, and Billy felt the tears he had been fighting spill over. Ignoring them, he bent forward, lifted his free hand, and touched Marcy's face. She smiled and, using his arm as a guide, slid her fingers up over his shoulder, across his chest, and up to his chin, turning her face toward his as if she could see him with her eyes. Her fingertips rested lightly on his chin, not moving, barely in contact, while her head tilted sideways again, questioningly.

"She wants to look at you now," said Arlene thickly. "But she's been taught not to do it without permission. Nod to tell her it's okay."

Billy nodded and closed his eyes as those gentle, sensitive fingers explored his face, encountered his tears, and hesitated. Marcy looked frightened and confused. She turned her head and seemed to be searching for the comforting presence of her mother.

Arlene took her daughter's free hand and spoke

as she signed into Marcy's palm. "It's all right. Daddy is happy to see you."

Marcy smiled again, a huge, radiant smile, and it didn't take words for Billy to understand that she was happy too.

When she had explored his face and shoulders, she made him stand, so she could measure herself and her mother against him. She touched his hair, then her own, and smiled again. Then she drew one of his hands and one of Arlene's to her face and leaned her warm cheeks against the backs of their fingers. To his amazement, she spoke aloud in a toneless, husky voice. "Dad-dee. Mar-cee. Mom. Good."

The three-way embrace was long and deeply emotional, and Billy whispered to Arlene, "Oh, babe, thank you! Nothing in my life has been better than this moment, not even seeing Holly being born."

Later, in the car, he returned to that moment. "In a way, when Marcy spoke and said what she did, it was as if, for her and me, our relationship was in the process of being born. How long will it take me to learn to talk to her?"

Arlene smiled and blinked hard. She had shed enough tears for one day. "That depends on how badly you want to learn."

He placed his right hand on the seat, where she could reach it and turned briefly toward her, his gaze burning with determination. "I want it bad, Arlie. I want to be able to tell her I love her. Tomorrow when I see her again. So teach me. Now. I can drive one-handed."

"Then you'll do it like this." With trembling fingers, she spelled out the words "I love you" against Billy's palm, again and again, until he clenched his fingers around hers and turned her hand over. "I love you," he spelled into her palm as he whispered the words aloud. "Now, how do I say 'Arlene'?"

THIRTEEN

Crash! Thud! Arlene woke up from a restless sleep and sat erect. What was that? Another thump and a muffled curse came from the direction of the living room of the big hotel suite she was sharing with Billy.

Not turning on a light, she slid out of bed and cautiously opened her door a crack. It was pitch dark, and the thudding continued along with muttered cries of pain. If it was Billy back from the walk he'd insisted he needed after their late dinner, and the few, provocative dances they'd shared, why didn't he turn on a light? She wondered sickly for a moment if the stresses of the day had sent him to the bar, but then told herself he would be able to resist doing that.

If it was a burglar who had broken in, why didn't he have so much as a flashlight to guide him as he went about his night's work?

Carefully closing her door, Arlene turned on the overhead light and stood still until her eyes were adjusted. Then, without warning, she flung the door wide, knowing that whoever was out there would be blinded as light flooded into the dark room!

She stared at the sight that met her eyes, not a drunk, not a burglar dazzled by light, but a man bent forward, clutching his left shin, rubbing it,

193

then standing erect and walking deliberately—and blindly—toward the other side of the room.

"Billy!" she whispered sharply. "What in the world are you doing?" She shook her head in despair, knowing the stupidity of asking. She knew what he was doing, and knew why, and it broke her heart to see him so.

It was as if he not only couldn't see her, but couldn't hear her either. He continued to fumble his way around the room, a dark cloth tied tightly over his eyes to block out whatever illumination might have come from the cracks around the drapes. He felt his way from a table to the wall, crashed his knees into the edge of a chair, and cursed again, bending to rub his bruises. He was barefoot, and shirtless, as if he had gone to bed and then arisen only to drag on pants and come out to experiment with a reality he could never really understand.

"Billy, stop it! You're going to hurt yourself," she said, ignoring the fact that he already had.

Running to him, she snatched the blindfold from his eyes and wrapped her arms around him, hugging him tightly. "Don't," she said. "Oh, don't!" But she remembered the times she had done the same, trying to learn what it must be like to be Marcy.

"Leave me alone," he said, turning from her, and as he spun away, she saw the plugs he'd inserted into his ears.

Grasping his arm, she dragged him back and pulled out first one, then the other, tossing them onto the desk, where they bounced and rolled to the carpet. "This doesn't help, Billy! It does her no good, and you a lot of harm. There's no point in trying. You'll never know what it's like to be deaf and blind!"

"I need to know," he said, his voice raspy. "Or how can I begin to understand her?" He strode away and flung back the drapes. "Look out there! See the beauty? The lights? The pulsing life that exists? It's the city she lives in, but does she even know it's there?" He came back to Arlene, his eyes wild, angry, his face drawn with pain.

"I walked for miles tonight, thinking about her, about her frustrations, about what it must be like for her," he said. "She can't see what I see, hear what I hear, know what I know! And I can't feel what she feels. I closed my eyes and tried to find the courage to cross a street. But even when I heard the traffic stop, I was scared to try it without first taking a tiny peek. I felt so guilty and so cowardly, because my daughter can never, ever, take a peek to see if it's safe. And then I remembered that she can't hear either! She wouldn't even have that to tell her she can go!"

He clasped Arlene's shoulders and threw back his head, asking in an anguished voice, "How can she ever go for a walk by herself? What does she do when she needs to be alone to think? She's never seen a sunset, a rainbow, a thunderhead! She doesn't know that her eyes are gray like yours and her hair as dark as mine and that she has the most beautiful smile I've ever seen. Maybe you were able to teach her how to use her smile, and when, and why, but no one can ever tell her what gray really is, or green or blue or red, or what a city looks like at night, or a sailboat in the wind. She's never seen the ocean, never seen a mountain. She hasn't heard a song or a bird or the splash of a waterfall.

"Oh, God, Arlie, her life must be so empty. I want to fill it for her! I want to give her all the things she's never had, and I know I can't, and it's killing me! I want to hold her and tell her I'm sorry, so sorry, for what happened to her, and that if there were any way I could change it, I would. It hurts so bad, knowing all the things she has to miss, all the things I can never give her." He lowered his head, shaking it slowly.

"Billy, don't think about those things, love," she said, gripping his wrists tightly, her heart aching for him. "Think about what she does have, what she has experienced.

"Even if she's never seen one, never heard one, she's *felt* the icy cold splash of a waterfall. She's hiked up a mountain, so she knows they're steep and rocky. And she skis down them. You saw her do that. She's felt the grass and smelled it, rolled in it, hid in it. She loves flowers because the petals are smooth and the scents delicious. She swims in the ocean and tastes it, compares it to lakes and rivers and knows they are all different from each other and from the bathtub. She knows the city is different at night. The vibrations under her feet are less with fewer cars and trucks on the road.

"She dances, Billy! She can feel the music in the air, in the floor, in her partner's movements. Of course there are things she hasn't done, will never do, but she is a happy, fulfilled young woman, and I will not permit you to feel sorry for her!"

"But Arlie—"

"No, dammit! She doesn't need your pity! She doesn't need you to break your bones and good hotel furniture trying to learn what her life is like. Her life is hers. Yours is something she can't comprehend, either, but that's because you are male and she is female. Can you say you know what it's like to have a baby because you've seen someone else have one?"

"That's not the same thing, dammit! *She'll* never see her own babies. She'll never hear them cry or laugh or call her mama! She'll never hear a man say I love you, or see his face when she says it to him. If she does."

"She will, Billy."

"Will she?" he said bitterly. "It's not fair, Arlie!" He dragged her against his chest, burying his face in her hair. "Oh, hell, it's so damned unfair, I want to go out and do permanent injury to someone for letting this happen!"

"If only you could know the progress she's made, see how she's grown and changed and matured, you'd have no fears for her."

"Then tell me," he said, stroking her hair back from her face, pressing her cheek to his bare chest. "Talk to me, Arlie. Give me all your memories of her growing up. Let me be part of her life." He touched her face again with a gentle hand. "And yours."

She drew in a tremulous breath, and found it filled with his musky scent. She tried not to breathe too deeply, not to be affected by the warmth and strength and closeness of this man she wanted with every pore of her body.

This was worse than the torture of the dances they had shared that night. Now, instead of being fully dressed, she was wearing a nightgown. Even though it was cut full, high-necked, and long-sleeved, her breasts were unfettered within it, and its flannel was old and thin. She was much too aware of Billy's bare chest, the feel of the crisp spirals of hair under her cheek, the slow, heavy rhythm of his heart. She knew she should push herself out of his arms, but right now she needed to be held as much as he did.

"Her life will be as full as anyone's is," she said quietly. "She will have everything, all the things you and I want for her. It may be a little more difficult for her, but she can do it. You have to have faith in her. I do."

"There are so many years that are a blank to me. So much time I didn't share with you both. God, I feel so cheated!" he said, leading her to the couch and sitting down, still holding her close.

"Oh, Billy. You don't know how much I wanted to tell you, wanted you to be part of our lives, but I *couldn't!*" She lifted her head from his chest and looked at him, pleading silently for understanding.

"I know. I'm not blaming you. What you believe to be true was more than enough reason to keep me in the dark, and you were protecting me from knowing about my mother. I know that, and I love you for it, but there's no longer any need for secrecy. Tell me."

She talked and he questioned for nearly two hours, and when she fell asleep, he continued to sit, holding her for more precious moments. Then, lifting her gently, he carried her into her room and slid her back into her bed. He paused at the door, his hand on the light switch, and turned to look at her.

"You're so wrong about us," he said softly, as if she would hear him in her sleep and maybe come to believe. "Our only relationship is that of a man and woman who need each other, a man and woman who belong together."

As if she had heard, she drew in a deep sobbing breath and let it out silently. He watched a single tear form in the corner of her eye, spill over, and run down to leave a tiny spot of moisture on her pillow. With a groan he turned off the light, closed the door softly, and opened the bedroom drapes to let in the city light and the faint sheen of the sliver of moon. Slowly, he walked back to the bed. Then, removing his pants, he climbed in beside her, sliding his legs down the length of hers.

"Just for a little while," he whispered, putting his arm over her and drawing her slowly into the curve of his body. With a sigh of pure pleasure, he breathed in the scent of her skin and gazed at her, loving the sight of her hair shining on the pillow beside him, the curve of her cheek, the point of her shoulder, the indentation of her waist and the rising curve of her hip. "I need to hold you, baby, and I'll be gone before you wake."

"This is my father, Bill Culver," Billy said to her, and Arlene sagged back against the porch rail as relief washed over her. The man looked exactly like Billy! There could be no doubt that he was who Billy claimed he was, and no more doubt that she had been wrong all these years. Nothing, nothing stood in her and Billy's way!

"Oh, I'm glad! So glad!" She flung her arms around Billy, and she realized for the first time that he was nude. He held her close to him, his warmth enfolding her, and she crowded into a tighter embrace, unable to get near enough.

She knew she should be embarrassed to be seen like this with him in front of a stranger, even one who was his father, who had released them both from the purgatory of believing they were related. But somehow, she wasn't. It was too good knowing that Billy had been right all along. She had wanted to believe him, had come so close to it, yet always there had been that tiny element of doubt, that question in her own mind, "what if?" Those doubts were gone now, and Billy was brushing his lips slowly over hers, and she couldn't have turned away from him for anything.

His hard arousal pressed against her leg and she moved, deliberately tantalizing him, rubbing her body on his, wishing she were as nude as he, so that they could be together completely. . . .

Arlene awoke, slowly becoming aware of something tickling her cheek and temple, of a familiar scent, a heaviness across her waist, and heat. . . .

It was a deep, coiling heat that curled and licked at her lower abdomen, the core of her womanhood, sending little tremors of sexual excitement down her legs, and upwards to her nipples, even though they were already painfully hardened. It was a good pain, a wonderful one, and she didn't want it to stop. It fluttered in her stomach and tightened her throat as she came fully awake, eyes popping open, to gaze confusedly into Billy's ardent eyes glittering in the faint light that shone through the window of her dark hotel bedroom.

"What . . . are you doing?" she asked.

"Waking you up," he said, his quick smile coming and going in his eyes. "I couldn't stand it another minute. You've been driving me slowly insane, moaning and moving against me for the past five minutes until I'm ready to explode. Either do it, Arlie, or move away. Please."

Do it? "Do what?"

His laughter was taut and throaty, deep and brief, but it vibrated right through her body, leaving her tingling all over. "Make love to me, Arlie."

She opened her mouth to speak, but no sound came out. She could only gaze into the glitter of his eyes. She tried to move away, but something held her very still, scarcely breathing, her heart beating too hard in her chest.

"Why are we in the same bed?" she managed to whisper.

"We were talking. You fell asleep. I brought you in here and then I just wanted to hold you for a while. I didn't mean to fall asleep. And I didn't mean to wake up like this." He didn't have to move his hips against her inner leg to show her what "this" meant, but he did. She shuddered, and her nipples tightened to aching beads. He slid one hand up her front and cupped a breast, smiling again as that nipple jutted into his palm. She gasped, her stomach contracting in another prolonged quake of pleasure. "I didn't mean for you to wake up like this either.

"But we both did," he continued, his gaze never leaving hers, "and everything I do from this moment onward, believe me, I mean. All I ask is that you mean it too. Arlie—are you on the pill?"

"I . . . yes, but . . ." she breathed, and licked her dry lips, watching his sultry gaze follow the motion of her tongue.

"Good. With you, I don't want anything between us."

"Billy . . . we . . . can't."

"Can't we?"

"No! Oh, no."

She swallowed hard and quivered again as he moved his hand gently over the curve of her breast. She ached to feel it, not through the flannel of her gown, but on her skin. She felt a rosy flush rising up her neck and knew he recognized it for what it was.

"Yes! Oh, yes," he countered mockingly. His smile faded, to be replaced by fierce, solemn intent as his thumb stroked her nipple. The tip of his tongue skimmed her lower lip, tracing the path her own had made.

"It isn't true, what you believe," he said in a soft tone of total conviction when he lifted his head to meet her eyes, dazed and filled with need. "My father was William T. Culver. I've seen his picture. I've seen the marriage certificate. I've heard over and over again the story of how he left to find work and somehow forgot to come back. Arlie, love, he existed then. Maybe he even exists now. Believe me! Please, believe me."

She wanted to slide away from him, but her muscles lacked strength and her resolve had been weakened, not only by the dream that Billy's father really did exist, but by the desire thundering through her blood. She wanted to move away, but she wanted more to believe in what Billy said.

Her nightgown was bunched up around her waist. Her left leg was hooked over Billy's right knee. One of her arms was squashed beneath her, and the other was tucked under his, over his waist.

She continued to look at him. His eyes darkened with yearning as he lifted himself away from her, and let her fall back onto the pillow. Then he bent his head and brushed his lips over her face and down under her chin, leaving a tingling sensation the length of her throat.

She drew in a shuddering breath. "Don't," she said after a moment. "Oh, God, Billy, we can't . . ."

"We are," he said, his voice a deep rumble. "We have to. Can you stop us?"

She tried to. She lifted one heavy arm to push him away, but it looped around his neck. She opened her mouth to tell him he had to leave, but somehow her parted lips sought his instead. Heat exploded in her loins as his tongue swept into her mouth. She cried out softly, pulling her lips free as, nipples aching, she pressed her chest against his and opened her legs to cradle his body. Her nails raked down his back as she arched into him, up to him, feeling the strength of his arousal and moving her nakedness against it. "Now, Billy! Right now!" she demanded, reaching for him, positioning him, seeking the fulfillment only he could give her.

"Arlie! Arlie!" He plunged into the slick, hot wetness that waited him, taking her in one swift lunge. He reared his shoulders back, arched, and drove again, deep into the tightness of her, his eyes squeezed shut, every muscle vibrating with tension and the agony of pleasure. He opened his eyes to look at her as she writhed beneath him, her legs clinging to his waist, her nails digging into his buttocks. Her hips rose to match his thrusts, and head thrown back, she cried out. He held her, pounding into her, and she cried out again, and again, the last time in triumph. Then it was over as fast as it had begun, they lay there entwined, staring at each other in awe, and in love.

Wavelets of aftershocks washed through Arlene, contracting inner muscles. Billy closed his eyes and buried his face against her shoulder, rocking her tightly against him.

"Are you all right?" he said moments later.

"I'll never be the same again."

She felt his smile against her cheek as he half lifted his head, decided he lacked the strength, and put it back down again. "Neither will I. Do you care?"

"About never being the same again? No. Oh, no."

Long moments passed while they stroked each other, finding warm nests for hands and fingers, soft, scented places for lips and noses. It was a time for sharing sweet, gentle kisses, smiles just visible in the faint light, and quiet, happy whispers. Then slowly, the world began to intrude.

A siren screamed in the street far below. Horns honked as the city came back to life with the coming day. Thoughts of practical matters tried to intrude where only thoughts of each other had been, and neither was ready for that.

Keep the day away, Arlene pleaded silently, sliding her hands down Billy's back. She loved the hardness of muscles under the satin of pliant skin, and adored the way his eyes glowed into hers as he looked at her, not trying to hide his sensual pleasure in the feel of her hands against him.

"I want this time to last forever," he whispered, running his hands into her tangled hair, his thumbs massaging her temples slowly, tenderly. "I never want to let you go."

It was what she wanted, too, more than anything, but it was what could never be.

Except . . . right now.

"Remember our spaceship?" she asked, her mouth trembling.

He placed a careful kiss over her lips. "I remember. Our secret place, where we traveled to wonderful worlds, met incredible beings, learned unbelievable things."

"Let's go back there, Billy, if only in our imaginations. No one ever found us there," she said shakily, and he knew what she meant. She wanted this time they were stealing to be their own private journey into a space that was exclusively theirs. No intruders, not even errant thoughts, were to be allowed to enter the world they were about to create. Heaven would have to forgive them for taking one day to love each other and be together.

"Billy," she murmured, using the words of childhood for a very adult request. "Let's pretend."

"Yes," he said. "Like before." His eyes shone. "Today we'll explore new worlds together, Arlie. And no one will find us, no one will know. This day is ours, my darling. Ours alone."

"Yes." Her eyes shone, too, with tears she refused to shed.

"I'm going to do something now I've always wanted to do," he said, changing the mood with his quick, naughty grin. He looked so like the Billy of old that her throat tightened, and she could scarcely force out the words. "What's that?"

He didn't reply, just got up on his knees between her legs and grasped both sides of the placket at the front of her nightgown. With one quick motion he ripped it straight down to the hem, laughing at the shocked expression on her face. "The conqueror!" he crowed, flinging the sides of her gown aside. He caught her bared breasts in his hands and buried his face between them.

Linking her hands behind his head, she pressed his whiskery face to her, loving the prickle and rasp of it. "And now that you've conquered me, hero, what do you plan to do? Or was that the entire act?"

"That was the preliminary. Now, I'm going to love you real, real slow, Arlie. Slow and so sweetly you'll never forget what it's like to be loved by Billy Culver, Conquering Hero, Master of the Spaceways, Commander of the Ship."

His fierceness, his confidence, even his arrogance delighted her, and she laughed with joy.

He caught his breath at the beauty of her sparkling, tear-spangled smile, and his heart filled to overflowing as she hugged him powerfully.

"I never have," she whispered, her laughter fading as she met his ardent gaze. "In all those years, Billy, I never once forgot."

As her tears spilled, he bent and caught her face between his hands, licking the drops from her temples.

He kissed her for a long moment, leaving her aching and afire, then lifted his head to smile at her. "After I'm finished showing you how perfect it will be slow and sweet, I'll give you hard and fast again, or maybe hard and slow—think of that! And then, when we're all rested up, I'm gonna let you do it to me, any way you want, for as long as you want, because you are my one true love and we're going to get better and better together, I promise."

"Promises never got anybody anywhere," she said breathlessly, pretending his kisses hadn't affected her in the least. "Action is what counts."

"Action is what you'll get," he said, moving against her. His eyes closed as he drew one of her already taut nipples into his mouth. She gasped with pleasure and the time for fooling around was over. Locking her arms behind his back, she rocked her hips against him. Passion soared higher and hotter within them until neither could withstand the need to be joined. Without awkwardness, as if they had been loving each other like this all their lives, they united their bodies. Arlene released a low moan of ecstasy, and Billy let out a growl of satisfaction. Their gazes locked, each reading the deep delight in the other.

"Mine," he said, and that said it all.

FOURTEEN

"It's breakfast time," Billy said much later when they awoke again and discovered it was fully daylight. A weak yellow sun shone on the water of Lake Washington, turning it as blue and sparkly as Billy's eyes. "You shower while I call downstairs for food."

She wrapped her arms around his neck. "Who's hungry?"

"You," he said, "are going to need your strength." Then, with a grin, he added, "And so am I. Have you always been so eager?"

With a glorious smile, she laughed and said, "Never! But I've never felt about anyone the way I feel about you, Billy. I think you're a bad influence on me."

"Yup," he said proudly. "Always have been. Always will."

For a moment they lay gazing into each other's eyes, both silently wondering what chance they had for "always," and both knowing it was slim to none. But their day was not over, and they refused to let those thoughts interfere with their loving.

"Get that shower warmed up, woman. I plan to join you in there in no more than three minutes."

She got out of bed, dragging the sheet with her, wrapping it around her body. "What's this?" Billy asked. "Hiding from me?" He caught the tail end of the sheet and snatched it away, leaving her standing there, wide-eyed, not knowing what to cover first, and finally deciding to cover nothing. She liked the way he looked at her.

In spite of the way he'd looked at her, it took a bit more than three minutes for him to join her.

Levering himself out of bed once he heard the sound of water thundering into the tub, Billy reached for the phone. It wasn't to order breakfast, but to call Glenn Klemchuck.

"I want my will changed," he said without preamble, and then went into detail. "Yes," he said impatiently when Glenn questioned his judgment. "Whether we are married or not. Arlene is from this day forward to all intents and purposes my wife. I want my copy here, ready for signature, no later than three this afternoon. Fly it up yourself if you need to, but get it here. To the hotel manager's office, not my suite. And then I want a detective. I want the best, and I want him yesterday. . . ."

When he was done, he pressed the button on the phone that connected him with room service.

Then he ordered breakfast.

"Took you long enough," she said, pretending to pout when he joined her in the shower ten minutes later.

He grinned. "But you waited."

She shrugged. "I didn't have any place to go."

"I called Glenn," he said. "I told him that the boat yard is to go into Lockyer Bay. You and I may get a little more noise at our end of the island, a little more dust during road construction, and we may be able to see some of the housing development. Are you sure that's what you want? I can change it with a phone call. I can, if you tell me to, cancel the entire deal."

She looked at him sharply. "And do what?"

"Oh, who knows? Sell it to some rich guy for a few million and live for the rest of my life off the proceeds. Do like I said the other day and give it to you as a wedding present."

She winced. "I won't be getting married."

"Or," he said as if she hadn't interrupted, "I simply could keep the land myself and leave the Island unchanged, the way it's always been."

She swallowed hard, thinking about the Island and how it had always been. First, when her ancestors came, it had been wilderness. Slowly, they had carved out a corner from forest and rock and built a house and planted gardens. Then others had come, cleared more forest, built more houses. The bridge was constructed to link the Island to the mainland. A road became necessary to move goods and people.

"Oakmount Island has always been changing," she said finally. "The changes have been so gradual, though, that most people hardly noticed. Maybe it's time for something they will see, Billy, time for some freshness, some activity, some progress and new blood. And there's room for what you've planned as well as for what already exists. I don't want you to cancel the development."

"Good. Because I stand to make a lot of money from it."

"And do a lot of good for a lot of people."

He shrugged carelessly. "Okay, so there'll be a few more jobs for locals. But that wasn't what was on my mind when I first conceived of the idea, don't forget. I just don't want you getting the notion that I've suddenly become a sterling character, or anything like that. I'm still the same old Billy Culver."

She moved suggestively against him. "It's your motives now that count with me."

His grin was all Billy. "Eager," he scoffed. "Did I say eager? What about greedy?"

"Complaining?"

"Never!" he said, lifting her, parting her legs around him and plunging deep within. "I'll teach you to be more than greedy. I want you avid. I want you ardent. I want you downright grasping."

Eagerly, greedily, she grasped him, and they moved in a steamy dance until his legs gave way and they slowly slipped, but still together, to the bottom of the tub.

"Dammit, Arlene, you told me you're on the pill! The only reason our society has such a taboo about incest is the risk of pregnancy. Since there is no risk of that, I don't see who the hell it would be hurting. Not that I buy into your suspicion for even one second, but since you believe it's a possibility, you tell me who it would be harming."

"Me," she said succinctly, and tried again to open the car door. Before she completed the motion, he used the electric lock on the driver's side and sealed her in again.

"This is kidnapping," she said. "It's illegal confinement!"

"So sue me!" He kept his finger on the door control, rendering hers useless.

"Let me out, Billy. We've gone over and over the same territory. I'm tired of it. I want to be alone. I want a chance to start forgetting."

"Forgetting? You think you're going to forget any more than I am?"

"No, I don't think I'm going to be able to forget. I'd like to try, is all, try to forget that we did something I knew—and know—to be terribly, horribly wrong! I let myself be swayed by feelings I should have controlled, and now I have to pay for that."

"Oh, sure!" He ran his hands through his hair. "I'm supposed to let you go inside all alone so you can spend the rest of your life castigating yourself for committing what you consider to be the dire sin of incest? I'm supposed to turn my back on you when you're feeling about as low as a slug? I'm supposed to let you take all the guilt onto your own shoulders and do nothing to try to alleviate it? I love you! I'm not going to let you beat your head into this brick wall any longer. What we did was not wrong! What we did hurt no one! What we did was our business and no one else's! Accept that. Believe that. We were entitled."

"We weren't entitled. What we did was wrong by anybody's standards, and the fact that we weren't creating a human life doesn't make it all right. What I did was wrong because I permitted myself to forget that there may well be a good reason why I shouldn't have done it. It's not so bad for you, because you don't believe what I do."

"Damned right I don't! And I never will."

"Ah, Billy, we had our day." Her gray eyes swept over his face, pleading for understanding. "We can't continue to take what isn't ours to have. Let me go. Please. I've had enough." She smiled, a small twisting of her lips that tore at his heart. "Like Holly says, 'time out.' Please, Billy, I need a time-out."

Looking at her pinched white face, the circles of exhaustion under her eyes, he was ripped by remorse. "Baby, I'm sorry," he said as he relented. Unlocking the doors, he opened his and got out, and took her overnight bag from the trunk and carried it to the door for her.

"Thank you," she said, and reached for her bag, but he refused to relinquish it. He took it inside and set it at the bottom of the stairs before turning to her.

"Come here," he said, holding out his arms. "Just for a minute, Arlie. I have things to say, and I'll say them easier if you're in my arms."

"Oh, Billy," she murmured, going to where she most wanted to be in the world, resting her head on his shoulder, feeling the strength of his arms as they enfolded her. "Why are we doing this? It's over. It has to be over. I can't let what we have together seduce me again."

"It's all right, love," he said, "I'm not going to seduce you or coerce you or do anything more than hold you like this, like a friend. I need this, too, you know. I know our being together would only cause you more hurt, and that's not what I want. But it isn't over between us. It will never be over." His strong fingers trembled against her jaw as he tilted her face up to his. "Somehow, we're going to find a way."

She searched his eyes, finding promises there that she knew he shouldn't make, that she knew she shouldn't want to believe. "I hope so. But in the meantime . . ."

"In the meantime, yes, I'll leave you alone." He frowned. "I'll try. It's not going to be easy."

She shook her head and swallowed hard. "No. No, it's not. That's why we have to . . . keep apart."

She watched his Adam's apple jump. "Here, on the Island, of course. But what about when we go to see Marcy?"

She smiled. "When we go to see her, we'll take her little sister along."

"Oh, baby," he groaned, tightening his hold on her for a moment. "Our girls, together! And us. Arlie, it's going to work. It has to!" Clasping her head in both hands, he tilted her face up.

"Promise me you'll wait," he said with savage demand. "Promise you won't let anyone come between us while I search for my father." He squeezed his eyes shut for a second, then glared at her, wild turbulence flaring in the blue depths of his

gaze. "I can't bear to let you go! I can't stand thinking that we might never have another day like
today! I'll die if you ever let someone else take my
place!"

"I won't," she said softly, hugging him tightly. "I
promise! I'll wait forever if that's what it takes for
us to be together again." She hesitated, started to
say something else, then closed her mouth, feeling
it tremble.

"Ah, babe, you can ask the same of me! I promise
too." Gently, he kissed her lips, her eyelids, her
cheeks, then let her go, sliding his hands down her
arms to her fingers, holding her by their tips as he
stepped back from her.

"I never slept with Ellen, you know. Or anybody
else, since I saw you again. I belong to you."

"I . . . belong to you." She repeated his words as
if they were exchanging vows, then slipped her fingers free. "Good night, Billy."

"Good night, Arlie. And thank you." He smiled
in response to her silent question. "Thank you for
Marcy, for our day together, for being you. But most
of all for your promise." With another smile, he
turned and left, his fingers in his hip pockets, palms
facing out as he ran lightly down the stairs to the
driveway.

From her position in the open doorway, Arlene
watched him go and heard him whistling softly as
he walked away.

It wasn't until she was in bed that she realized
he'd forgotten his car in front of her house. Billy,
forgetting his precious BMW? Maybe, she thought,
that was what love did to a man.

Then she turned over and buried her face in her
pillow, letting her tears flow.

Because that was what this kind of love did to a
woman.

• • •

Of course he came back, remembering that he'd left his car in her driveway. He pounded on her door, calling her name. When she came downstairs and opened the door, he claimed he'd left his keys on her hall table and didn't want to ruin her reputation by leaving his car outside her house all night.

It was then that he saw she'd been crying and took her into his arms to comfort her.

She was still crying when he carried her up the stairs and stood her by her bed. Her sobs continued unabated, but softly, as he tugged her nightgown off over her head and laid her on the tumbled sheets. Her tears moistened their sweet, yearning kisses, but her arms held him as tightly as his held her while they loved each other yet again, for one last time.

"My darling, don't," he murmured when it was over and still she wept. "Tell Marcy I love her. Tell her I'll be back when I can make it right for all of us."

"All right," she whispered, and he touched her face with tender lips.

"You knew, didn't you?" he said. "And that was why you were crying?"

She nodded. "I knew we couldn't stay in the same place and not . . . do this."

"And that when we did, you'd feel like this, and that I wouldn't be able to stand it, so I'd have to leave."

Again, she nodded. "Please, go now, Billy."

He got out of her bed, slowly pulled his clothes on. "I'm coming back."

She looked at him sadly. "Yes." She didn't believe him.

He left then, not whistling, and she lay there, no longer crying.

From across the water came the faint scream of a huge saw blade as the mill's newly reinstated second shift produced lumber for the housing project.

That night was the last time Arlene cried.

Now, two months later, with the kitchen door open to the warmth of a late April morning, Arlene thought she heard the scream of the saw again. Heavy trucks rumbled to and fro along the road that skirted Billy's property near the end of the bridge, disappearing into the forest, and swinging back toward the water, just visible from where she stood.

"Is the coffee on? Boy, am I ready for my break!"

June Maybee's voice startled her, and she wheeled around quickly, catching the edge of the counter as dizziness assailed her.

"Good heavens, sit down," said June, grabbing her arm and shoving her into a chair. "Look at you!" June went on, wrapping her fingers around Arlene's wrist with plenty of room left over. "Here, have a brownie. You're getting positively anorexic." She opened the plastic container on the table and placed it close to Arlene.

"I'm not hungry," she said, pushing the box away. The sight of the rich, sweet squares made her feel sick, but that wasn't surprising. Everything made her feel sick. She sipped her coffee. It was hot and strong and she could tolerate it, if not much else.

"What's wrong?" June planted her hands on her hips and looked down at Arlene. "Come on, we've been friends a long time, Arlene. You saw me through my messy divorce, and gave me a job so I could feed my kids when Phil didn't come through with support. So now it's time for me to return the favor if there's any way I can. Tell me what's wrong. Let me help."

Arlene shook her head. "You can't help. No one can. It's something I have to work out for myself."

June gave her a skeptical look. "You're not doing a great job." She busied herself at the counter for a moment or two with a stack of construction-paper stars, then without looking at Arlene, she said, "By the way, when is Billy Culver coming back?" She spun around in time to watch what little color Arlene had fade.

Arlene lifted her chin and met June's gaze levelly. "What makes you think he has anything to do with the way I feel?"

June poured herself a cup of coffee, pulled a chair out from the table, and sat down. "He left," she said, then bit into a brownie.

Arlene shrugged and looked out the window. "Yes, he did, didn't he?"

"Wasn't that strange, his taking off like that, after making such a fuss about Holly going to school here? Have you had any more letters from her?"

Arlene was careful not to show anything of what she felt. "No, nothing further. Just that one letter. I guess she's busy, back in Phoenix."

"Is Billy coming back?"

"June, I really don't have any knowledge of Billy's plans."

"Okay, then, if it's not Billy, is it Sam and Ellen? I know you were as surprised as anyone when they up and got married and moved to Mexico like that."

Arlene gave an astounded laugh. "God, no! I think that's fine. Astonishing, maybe even ludicrous, considering how dissimilar they are, and probably immoral, considering their doctor-patient relationship, but I don't have any problems with what they did. I wish them both well," she added, getting to her feet.

"Good," June said. "Remember, though, I'm here and I care about you."

Arlene squeezed her friend's shoulder and took her cup to the sink. "I'd better get back to work."

"Yeah. I suppose I should too."

"Sit still and finish your coffee."

"Arlene—" An urgent note in June's voice made her pause with her hand on the door leading from the kitchen and look back at her friend.

"Call him," said June softly. "Tell him how you feel."

Arlene drew in a sharp, shaky breath. "Call who?"

"Whoever you need to, before you end up in the hospital. People do die for love, you know. I don't want it to happen to you."

She felt a great thickness rise up in her throat, threatening to choke her. "June, don't . . . probe," she whispered.

"Then call him," said her friend again pleadingly. "Call him. He might be suffering as much as you."

"I . . . can't." Arlene swallowed hard, once, then twice, before she could speak again. "I can only wait for him to call me."

But the waiting went on and on.

And so did the pain.

Any late-night sound was always enough to set her heart clamoring inside her chest, and Arlene to wondering if it was the wind, or the rain, or an animal. Or maybe a footstep on her porch. This late night in mid-May was no different. A sound had wakened her, and Arlene lay rigid in her bed, waiting for whatever came next.

Too often it had been nothing. Too often she had lain there for what seemed like hours, only to drift back into an uneasy sleep, wondering if he would ever come back and earnestly telling herself no, he would not, that it was time to forget, time to pull herself together, time to . . . let go.

It was easier to deal with disappointment when you never expected anything good, she decided, but when the loud knock sounded on her door, her heart stopped for several beats before it resumed with a hard, tumultuous thudding.

Arlene tumbled out of bed, snatched up a robe, and nearly fell down the stairs. Jerking the door open, she stared at the man standing there, felt herself grow dizzy and faint, knew she was swaying and tried to catch herself.

"Dad . . ." she whispered. "Oh. Dad. You didn't say you were com—" Her eyes rolled back and she slumped toward the floor.

George Lambert caught her, lifted her up, and strode inside. He sat her on a chair, shoving her head down between her legs.

"Arlie, honey, I came as soon as Miss Quail told me how sick you are," he said when she was able to sit up again. "What is it, my dearest? What's happened to you? Oh, my Lord, are you pregnant again?"

She shook her head, her face obscured by her hair. He gently tilted her head up, and looked into her pale face. His concern at her emaciated condition was clearly visible in his expressive eyes. "You look terrible!" he said, examining her in the light from the fixture overhead. "What have you done to yourself? My God, Arlie, why didn't you let me know you were ill?"

"I'm not ill. I'm all right, Dad," she said weakly, then crumpled against him, her arms around his middle, weeping as if she would never stop.

When Arlene was calmer, he took her into the

kitchen and sat her at the table while he made a pot of tea.

"Now," he said presently, sitting across from her and sipping the strong, hot tea. "I know I haven't been much of a father to you, dear, but I do love you and to see you like this saddens me. If I can help in any way, please let me."

"There's nothing you can do, Dad, but I'm so glad you're here. I've never felt more alone in my life."

"You're not alone any longer, dear one. I'm here with you and I'll stay as long as you need me."

"Thank you, Dad. Oh, I want to tell you. I need to tell someone! I . . . just don't know where to start, and to tell you all of it, I'll have to include things you'll find painful."

George smiled. "I'm no stranger to that, dear, and I have very broad shoulders. So begin with what's important. What happened when Billy came home? How did it all go wrong for you again?"

She stared at him, gulped down her surprise, and asked, "Miss Quail told you he'd been back?"

He nodded. "I was glad for you. Considering the way you felt about each other when you were young, I'm surprised you didn't—find each other again."

She searched his eyes, wondering how much he knew. Obviously, nothing. "Glad?"

"Of course. If it was right for the two of you, I hope you didn't let my former disapproval of him have any bearing on your decision." He looked ashamed for a moment. "Forgive me, my dear, but when Myrtle told me how precipitously he'd left after having told everyone he meant to stay here, and how you went into an old-fashioned decline soon after, I had to draw the conclusion I did. That you turned him down."

She said nothing, only looked at the table. Her father clearly didn't know!

"Well? Was I right? Is that what happened?"

She drew in a shaky breath. "Some-something like that."

"And was it because of—past events?"

She nodded miserably.

"Do you know why I disapproved of him, Arlie?"

She nodded again, then frowned, trying to work through the massive confusion befuddling her brain. "At least, I thought I did." She looked at him searchingly, wishing she could guess at the depth of his knowledge about his father and Jenny. "Why did you?" she asked finally.

"Because of my own experiences. I made the mistake most parents make—hoping to protect my child from the hurts I had suffered. But maybe I was wrong. Maybe yours and Billy's backgrounds weren't as different as mine and your mother's. Maybe you would have made your union work better than we did."

He smiled a trifle sadly while Arlene looked at him, bewilderment swirling in her tired mind.

"Weren't you and my mother happy together? I never knew you had different backgrounds."

"We did. She was—this will sound dreadfully snobbish, my dear, but she was a barmaid when I met her." He rose, walked to the other side of the kitchen and stood leaning on the counter, facing Arlene. He smiled again. "It was, on my part, love at first sight. Of course, my parents disapproved tremendously and threatened to cut me off without a dime if I married her. At that point I didn't care, and we wed a week after I took my graduate degree and was offered a position with Carleton's archaeology department.

"She seemed happy at first, but of course she wanted more than I could provide, and the kind of travels I took her on, to very unexciting places, soon palled. She chose to stay behind after the first year.

She was also quite dismayed to learn that apart from paltry earnings from a few publications, and my stipend from the university, I had no income. If she wanted pretty baubles, she was going to have to work for them. My parents had meant what they said. They cut me off."

"I had no idea! I'm sorry. Did she leave you? I'd always thought she died. That's what you all told me when I was a child and—"

"Yes, she died. But after she'd left you and me. That's why my parents raised you, dear. She was still alive when I brought you here. She abandoned both of us." He sighed, and then went on.

"Arlene, the reason I was so adamant in sending Billy Culver away after his mother's death was that I'd been forced to admit that my parents were right about your mother, and I had been wrong. And when I made my decision to marry her, flawed as it was by love or lust or whatever drives a man to make bad judgments, I had been in my late twenties. You, my dear, were a girl of seventeen. I believed your judgment was even more imperfect than mine, so I banished the boy.

"I had suffered much at your mother's hands because we came from different social strata, had different expectations, different goals. I'm sure she suffered too. Don't think I'm putting the entire blame on her. But I feared for you if you wound up married to a young man who drank too much, ran with a bad crowd, and hadn't even completed high school. You hadn't been reared for that kind of life. You wouldn't have been able to adapt any more than Loretta was able to adapt to my kind of life."

She stared at him. "And that was your sole objection to Billy . . . for me?"

Slowly, he walked back to the table and stood with his hands on the back of his chair. "At the time, as I said, it seemed valid. Now, of course, it no longer is. You're an adult and can make your own decisions. So what is holding you back?"

She drew in a deep breath and let it out slowly, wishing she didn't have to tell her father this, but knowing that he had a right to know. Almost as great a right as Billy had. "Because Billy is, in all likelihood, your much younger half brother, Daddy. Grandpa and Jenny . . . produced him together. I'm so sorry," she said contritely, seeing the shock on his face. "I thought maybe you knew about it and that was why you didn't want me to fall in love with Billy."

George sat down hard and stared at her. "Oh, my dear one. Oh, my poor child! I hoped you would never learn of that old, sad affair." He shook his head slowly. "Did your grandmother know?"

"I'm sure she didn't."

"Thank God for that. How did you know?"

On her knees beside him, Arlene wrapped her arms around her father and explained about the letters. "There's no proof. I realize that, but the suspicion eats at me. It has since I first found the letters and realized that was the only logical explanation for Marcy's birth defects."

"The only . . . ? Arlene, my child, all you have is a suspicion? Have you spoken to a doctor about this? Not one of your therapists, my dear, but a geneticist! Someone who might be able to either confirm your suspicion or scotch it completely."

She got to her feet and returned to her chair, frowning. "No. No, of course not."

"Why, 'of course'? It should have been your first step!"

"In a way, it was. I mean, after I read the letters and came to the conclusion I did. I did ask my doctor if my being closely related to Marcy's father might have been the reason for her defects. He said it certainly could have, that it was even likely it had been."

"Did you tell him the degree of relationship you suspected?"

She shook her head. "He didn't ask and I was happy to let the subject drop. I didn't need to know more. What I knew was bad enough. Daddy, please understand how . . . ashamed I felt. Dirty. I'd broken a taboo, however unwittingly, and my daughter was the one to suffer. For a long time I felt I didn't really deserve to live but I had to because maybe that was my punishment."

"Arlene, you don't still feel that way, do you?"

"No. Or . . . I had stopped feeling like that, until Billy came back and we . . . I . . ."

He covered her hands with his. "I understand," he said, and she knew that he did.

"I may be wrong," he said then. "It could be simply that I hate to think my father would have been so dishonorable, but I find it extremely difficult to accept there is the remotest possibility he fathered Jenny's son."

"But what if he did? The possibility stops me every time I think of it. The fear it might be true, and that because it is, I am responsible for what happened to Marcy."

George sat looking at her thoughtfully for several minutes. He poured more tea, took a cookie from the bag June had left behind, and munched. Finally, he said, "For a long time you searched for a reason for what had befallen Marcy. Not unnaturally, you wanted something to blame. Only, there was nothing, no one. Then, when you found the letters, suddenly it all fell into place for you. If you and Billy were related, you had your guilty party. Yourself. And who better to blame for a child's ills than her mother? Society does it all the time. Why should you be any different? But, my dear, you failed to take into consideration the rules of consanguinity."

"The what?"

"The rules of consanguinity. Not legal rules, or even moral, but natural ones, genetic. If Billy had been *my* son, then yes, maybe your theory would hold water. But even then, the fact that you had different mothers would have provided a degree of separation, a degree of safety in the matter of genetics. Not that half brother and half sister should ever marry, of course. But in many jurisdictions, first cousins can and do, with no ill effects. And in your case, if what you believe is true, the degree of consanguinity is less than that.

"There are genetic tests, dear. You and Billy could both have them. If those tests show that the combination of your genes was indeed responsible for Marcy's problems, then you've lost nothing. However, they could well prove that there is nothing holding the two of you apart but a suspicion in your mind. Think about it, darling child. And then, maybe, act upon it. After all, what can it hurt?

"Now," he went on, getting to his feet with a change of subject, "I suggest we both get a little sleep. Is my bed ready, as it usually is? I'm more than ready for it."

"Of course it is." They walked up the stairs together, both silent and thoughtful. Outside her door, her father hugged her and told her not to lie awake, but to rest because tomorrow was another day.

The homey phrase brought new tears to her eyes. She blinked them away as she lay on her bed, hands behind her head, staring up at the ceiling, knowing she wouldn't sleep. But at least she had something different to think about, because what if . . .

As she lay waiting for daylight, without her even knowing it, sleep came stealing over her.

• • •

It was ironic, she thought later when she was capable of coherent thought, that she didn't hear a thing—not the crunch of gravel, nor the slam of car doors, nor the footsteps on her porch. She did, though, hear the heavy knocking on her front door and leapt up, certain she must have slept in and June was there already.

"Billy . . ." She shoved her hair out of her eyes as she stared at him, standing in the doorway, outlined against the dazzle of the sea. "Billy . . ."

"My God, but you're skinny!" he said, and then snatched her into his arms. "I found him, sweetheart! I brought him with me. Look. Arlie baby, lift your head and meet my father. Oh, God, Arlie, this is no time to cry, you dope." He sounded as if he were crying himself. "Don't you understand? It's all over! I found him!"

Dashing her tears from her eyes, she said, "I'm not crying, I'm laughing. I think."

He turned her toward the man who stood on the porch, gazing out over the Sound, as if embarrassed by their emotion. "Darling, this is William T. Culver. My father. Bill, turn around and meet my wife."

The man wore an ill-fitting suit that looked as if it belonged on someone much larger. His teeth, when he smiled, showed broken and black. He had only a thin fringe of pale hair, blond or gray, around a mostly bald head, and was a foot shorter than Billy and fifty pounds lighter. His skin was pasty pale, as if he'd been under a rock all his life, and his hazel eyes kept shifting away from hers. If there were any family resemblance, Arlene couldn't see it. Still, she looked at him and she *knew*. This was the right man.

She extended a trembling hand and gripped the one he obediently gave her in return. "Mr. Culver."

"Howdy," he said, blinking hard, squinting. "He

says I gotta show you the back of my neck." Without further ado, he crouched down, bent his head forward, and exposed his nape to Arlene. "See? The map of Montana, right there, plain as day. My boy, he's got it too. He says your girl has it." His voice, with his head bent forward as it was, came muffled.

"Yes," Arlene said in little more than a whisper. "That's right. My daughter has it too."

"Our daughter," Billy corrected her, then grinned. "Both our daughters." He picked Arlene up and spun her around and around, laughing uproariously, joyfully.

And that was how George found them when he came down the stairs to see who was kicking up such a ruckus so early in the morning.

"Bill really is my old man, Arlie," said Billy a long time later, propping himself on one elbow and smoothing back the tousled hair surrounding her face. They were sprawled on the hearth rug before the fireplace in his cottage. That was as far as they'd gotten on their journey to the bedroom before Billy's strong legs collapsed—along with his will to hold out until he had her in a bed.

"I didn't just bail out any old rubby-dub of the San Fernando jail and tell him he had to pretend to be my father. My detectives finally tracked him down there, and I pulled a bunch of strings in order to get him out."

He sighed. "The trick now, I think, is going to be keeping him out."

Arlene laughed softly. "The original Bad Billy Culver? The pattern from which you were cut?"

"Like father, like son. All bad. Rotten to the core."

"Oh, I don't know," she said with a lazy, satisfied smile. "I wouldn't call you *all* bad."

"No?" He nuzzled her neck. "What part of me do you think is good?"

"The way you make me feel is good."

"Yeah? When I feel you like this, I want to be bad."

"Oh, Billy," she said on a long breath. "Go ahead, my lover, my darling, my bad boy. Be bad with me! As bad as you like."

He slipped inside her, holding himself very still, eyes shining down into hers. "I want to make a baby in you, Arlie. I want to do it deliberately this time, to celebrate us."

"Yes!" she cried, wrapping him tightly with her arms and her legs and her love. "I went off the pill the day you left, waiting for this day. So give me a baby. Give me a boy. A big one, a bad one, one exactly like you!"

"Here he comes," said Billy exultantly, giving her what she longed for. "Bad Billy Culver, just for you."

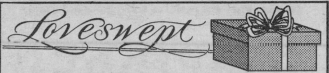

"Susan Johnson's love scenes sparkle, sizzle and burn!"--*Affaire de Coeur*

FORBIDDEN

by Susan Johnson
author of BLAZE

Brilliant, beautiful, and darkly exotic, Daisy Black displays her part-Absarokee Indian heritage with pride. She is an attorney in an age when few women work in such professions, and has come to Paris where she meets the Duc de Vec, an irresistibly handsome aristocrat. Fresh and untouched, Daisy challenges him intellectually, and she tempts him as no other woman ever has.

In a story rife with scandal and rich with sensuality, Daisy and the Duc flirt, fight, and ultimately flare up in the hottest and most enthralling novel Susan Johnson has ever written.

 THE SYMBOL OF GREAT WOMEN'S FICTION FROM BANTAM On sale now at your local bookstore.

AN 336 - 9/91